for D.M.

Kelly

A NOVEL

MICHAEL
MULLEN

Wolfhound Press

ISBN 0 905473 69 8

First published by
WOLFHOUND PRESS
68 Mountjoy Square, Dublin 1.

Published with the assistance of
The Arts Council (An Comhairle Ealaíon)

British Library Cataloguing in Publication Data

    Mullen, Michael
      Kelly.
      I. Title
      823'.914[F]   PR6063.U3/

      ISBN 0-905473-69-8

Cover design by Jarlath Hayes
Illustration by Jeanette Dunne
Typesetting by Redsetter Ltd.
Printed in Ireland

CHAPTER ONE

Kelly had one eye; a large, blue cyclopic eye which never slept. It stared, mesmerized at the world into which it had been born; bog and mountain and a bleak grey cloud sky carrying rain.

It was unbalanced by an impotent blue eye; withered and runty, a half-idiot twin. But in his twentieth year a maggot began to move in the shrivelled pupil, a white maggot the colour of leprosy. It suckled upon the black marrow of the eye fermenting into poison. In the dark cave it fattened into an ugly, corrugated monster. Strong enough to assert its hellish purpose, it tailed itself through the transparent membrane of Kelly's eye and poked about.

Kelly screamed and raved, ravaged. The countryside heard him roaring in the dark night, roaring that an end might be put to him, or the enemy within. He ran across the hills frothing, poulticing the eye with sods of turf, seaweed, cow-dung and horsedung to draw away the evil. It continued to feed and fatten, and fears were that Kelly would be consumed into a maggot, as if the cuckoo were to eat the nest she was reared in.

They brought the wisest hags and bent women from all over the County Mayo to look into the eye of the face of the upstanding body of Kelly which had been chained by Pakey Toughy to a standing stone, scotched with ogham script in a field. It stood close to the sinister, collapsed nipple of a fairy mound.

—The poor lad is doomed to an early grave, one lamented in her darkest wake voice.

——'Tis the devil himself, like the serpent in the garden, another added, outdoing the rest.

They muttered together over a skillet pot, hanging from a crook over a slow smouldering fire. Into the potato-porridge boiling pot they poured herbs, vegetables, berries, green weeds from the river, heather from the hills, brewed it into a buff slime, steeped it in yellow buck and bound it to the eye with strips of sacking. But it was a royal jelly for the bee. The maggot thrived and fattened and they feared for the life of Kelly.

The hags failed. They shuffled, humped, down the road and back along other roads to where they came from among bleak mountains, muttering half-understood prayers, and incantations. The power was leaving them.

No screed of relief for the declining Kelly. He was left bellowing, chained to a stone in a field, dragging heavy garments of iron about a knacker-yard carcass.

Everybody in the countryside was gathered in the village for the fair. Cowdung slop and talk, lowing of thin, mangy cattle, palm slapping signatures to bargain with. ——Put it there, and a half-crown for luck. I'm letting her go easy for twenty pounds and she the best heifer that ever cropped on Sliabh Gorta. You got me on a day and me feeling dacent. For nothing you're getting her.

Squeals of bonhams caged in cribbed carts, hauled by hind legs, smashed writhing into other creeled carts. Sodden mist and midden steam, mud churned into muck, mixed with hay and straw. Time, starved, dragging itself down the street, slow between houses and, beyond the houses, between stone walls. A jerky Time with no clock measure; patient for bargaining; racing merrily when sticks flew and knuckles cracked on jaws; wrapped in a warm blanket of talk in the public houses.

But above the market sound, the sound of Kelly, the maggot thriving like a healthy bonham in the jelly of his eye; feeding like a farrow, and the fear that it might grow large and independent and eat half the countryside.

The eldest and wisest men gathered in Flaherty's pub, thick glasses of porter in their hands, sulky eyed, and not surprised. This bleak countryside generated wild imaginations in which everything was probable. There was nothing abnormal about Kelly, a strange infliction, nothing more.

——A fellow beyond in Balla had worms and him thirty. His inside was like a sieve with them working their way through his liver and his intestines, even into his heart they said. They were seen to come out of his belly, old Tom Corley recalled. There was no surprise in his voice.

The listeners had their own stories to match Corley's about inflictions of rats and frogs in Shrule, Claremorris and Pontoon. They all had their own singular cures.

——This fellow I'm talking about, continued Corley, his name was Fahy, went to priest and doctor and neither prayers nor healing were any good. It was an old woman in Ballysalach who had a lot of the prayers and secrets brought to Ireland by the Fermorians, who finally cured him. A feed of potatoes with sulphur and brimstone in it. He's a fine healthy man to this day, married to one called Mangan. He'd still show you the traces of the worm holes.

And on it went and tangled, one story darker and stranger than the other. And all the time Kelly tore in torment out in the field.

The blacksmith Mickey O'Gara, a big lame-stepped man, hooped in silence, spoke. He had been injured somewhere in India in a battle.

——There is no cure other than fire, one of the four elements of the universe. I tried the pincers on the bugger's tail, and devil a stir from him. If he grows any bigger, he'll ate Kelly and consume the rest of us. The last time I tried to pull him out I saw he was growing feet. So he's starting to walk. I counted them. Ten pair of feet. He'll play hell I tell you.

——What were you going to say about fire? someone asked.

——I think we should bring Kelly down to the forge, strap him to the anvil, redden a poker and burn the monster out of his eye.

——It's very extreme, George Lavelle said.

——I'm telling you it's the only cure, take my word for it.

And he seemed to speak wisely, because he seldom if ever spoke. They talked on. Time was slow, and if they had not today, they had tomorrow and the morrow after it or early, rather than late, the night. So they ordered more drink and then more. It was midnight when all that Mickey O'Gara had said seemed logical and right. They felt strong: their vision was clear: purpose had hardened. They would rid the land of the Biblical infliction.

—We'll march up to the field and drag him down to the forge, the communal voice said.

They funnelled out in serious funeral gait, and re-assembled into a pool outside the pub. They went over their premises throwing in the rubble of talk to harden soft patches, and staggered up the town singing, slapping one another on the back, asking about wife and nephew and daughter, acres of land and bog banks. All good Christians were now in bed. Lights were out. A long ell of talk and song and raimeis. Everything was normal, for who is to strike a standard for normality here?

Kelly was groaning his guts out, no repose in his soul, twisting himself one way, then another, tearing at the chains, gnashing his fine white teeth. The exorcists approached.

They climbed across the ditch and into the field, O'Gara holding the torch for the faltering, fumbling figures. The stone wall crumbled away, rolling stone by rolling stone. Mickey O'Gara walked towards the middle of the field and discovered Kelly from the night. There was a carrion crow on the standing stone, evil-looking. They hooshed it away. It flapped, on witchy wings in dark humour across the moon.

—Poe's crow, someone remarked.

—Raven, a voice corrected.

—Poe's raven.

—She was standing on me head, picking at me eyes, Kelly groaned.

—Did she say anything? Mickey O'Gara asked.

—Ca, Ca, Kelly said.

—Maybe she was talking Irish, Tim Loftus remarked.

—I never heard of a crow speaking Irish, Mickey O'Gara said.

—Never mind about talking crows, Kelly groaned. Will somebody clean this crowshit from me head? She's been at it for the last three hours. It's running down me neck.

—God, Kelly, your head is thatched with it. There is the

manuring of half an acre there.

The long ten-legged maggot munched during the ramble of irrelevant conversation, stuffing itself like a cow in a cabbage garden. O'Gara held the torch to the maggot in the eye. It wriggled its tail, rumped itself in a horrid way, which would harrow honest men.

——A sight for sore eyes, John Creane said, stooping over to accommodate his seven-foot narrow frame.

——We could put a rope around its tail, and pull the devil out, Tim Loftus said.

——And let him escape into the fields? He'd ate every bullock and sheep in the county and maybe march on Dublin.

——If that's so, leave him where he is, leave him where he is, Liam Mulcahy cried.

——Oh Saint Patrick, Saint Brigid, Saint Fursey and all the saints of this island, alleviate this affliction, Kelly roared to the stars.

——I tell you crowd of doubting idiots that we'll only drive this plague out by fire. Watch this, Mickey O'Gara told them. He stuck the flaming brand to the maggot's tail. It trembled and twisted away from the heat.

——It couldn't be the devil or Beelzebub, seeing that fire is eating and drinking to them, commented a divine.

——Bring him down to O'Gara's forge, the communal voice counselled.

They pulled the chains from around the stone, hoisted them on their backs, and the manacled Kelly was led through the sleeping town. The rattle of chains was dragged across the dreams of decent people. The clanking and the clinking freed fiends tethered by good living in the cisterns of their souls. They twitched and sweated in their sleep at apocalyptic parades of leathered winged birds and reptiles, rampaging, rifling, running, rattling in a lurid landscape, twisting, seething, contorting with stinking-toothed grins in seas of burning salt, or limping on leather membrane batwings on a wild sky.

They reached the mouth of the forge through a valley of tangled iron, where rust fungus sucked the damp rain. Mickey O'Gara took the torch, flung it on the smouldering fire, fed it with turf and wet slack and pumped air into it through the

bellow's snout, its belly palpatating like a bullfrog. Flames
ran from the snout in vicious tongues through turf and slack.
O'Gara, with shirt sleeves tucked up, plunged a poker in the
fire. They bent Kelly backwards down, pillowed his head on
the shiny, beaten anvil and bound his body tight with chains.

—Hould him down. Hould him down, they roared at one
another.

Now the brand was ready. It glowed like a mystical sword
above their heads with raw, glowing virtue.

—Hould him, now, hould him now because he'll roar
something fierce.

O'Gara held the down-pointing brand a foot above the
rotted eye socket. Kelly gasped and writhed. He twisted
screaming for release. They dragged a cart axle across his
stomach, haltered his neck with the hoop of the anchor
from the good ship Benburb, and sat on him, faces looking
down on his face. The maggot began to vibrate and turn,
tossing its tail away from the heat.

—Let him have it quick, Mickey, they encouraged.

O'Gara, aiming, lunged forward at the maggot and the
slobber, plunging, twisting, blistering, charring at the corrupt-
ing, convulsing strange creature. The brand lodged in the eye.
Strength gushed from O'Gara's body, like a vomit, and he
collapsed on the floor, pale as death, vigour drained from
him.

As they grew old the story of what happened in O'Gara's
forge that night spawned and spread in different directions.
Some would recall the sizzling flesh of the shrivelling maggot,
its death screech, the putrid stench of smoke hissing up from
the eye. Others would speak of the Herculean strength
pumping and seething through Kelly's body, the heavy
knocking of his heart, like the banging of a madman on a
door. His mouth thrown open, screaming, gasping in all the
air in the forge and in the nearby fields, gulping an ocean of
it into pumping lungs. Others again would remember the
explosion of lightning from the pegged-eye socket, sawing a
hole in the sooty roof, the soul of the maggot evicted from
its habitat, and the thousand small voices like bitter imps,
running and dancing and whinnying outside the forge. And a
few others would speak of O'Gara, grey haired, old, tottering

before his time, too weak to talk; rheumy eyed; convulsed at memories; fear that horrid dreams might scale the weak ramparts of his imagination.

Peripheral figures. At the centre of the vortex, the sat-on-chained-Kelly, maggot meat.

With a wild blue eye spasming with fear, he saw the ranged brand, its searing comet plunge. An explosion of hot sparks in his mind, molten iron and ashes in his veins, running through him burning. Caught in the twisting turbulence, going inwards and down.

He entered a sea slime cave at the base of his mind, under a black roof, with running echoing pessimistic wine laughter, and past kennels where the mad dogs of his race were tethered. He stood at the door of a hall, twilit with fat-fed torches, throwing cumbersome, distorted shadows. Wild raucous laughter beating at his ear. His eyes grimaced firmness into the room. It was long, low, raftered, thatched. Dogs gnashed their teeth at him. Trampled bones with shredded meat matted into the floor. Acrid body sweat, salt sick tang of dirty sea bodies. Kelly now among his own with free knowledge, tearing free from nets thrown by the sacred hunters. Marrow, bone, nerve fattening, thickening, hardening.

He stood at the dwarfy, thick doors of his racepast, the brand still deep in his socket.

CHAPTER TWO

——Come to the top of the table, Kelly, you've been expected for the last five thousand years, and we are all cobwebbed with patience waiting for you.

Kelly, weak kneed, looked up through the half-lit smoke and murk at a tunn of bloated flesh, a leary mouth, and rolled back lips.

——Are you ailing with a wasting sickness? the lard tunn boomed again at the miniscule figure at the door, snarled at by hungry dogs.

Kelly stood, stuck in door mire, mad to rush half-blind from the presence of the immense mountain of flesh.

——Feed the brands, you dried up cross-eyed bitches, the lard tunn roared at the servant women with plate carrying faces. There was a mice run of fright and fidget through the low hall, as they searched for earthen tallow pots.

A quarrel seeded in the middle distance, two figures arching across oak, tearing long hair, flesh, hide, and eyes. A bunchy dwarf pumped up clenched fists into the face of an opponent. A swing of a decorated bone club caught him on the mouth; a gush of buck teeth and sputum, on to the table, a tearing yelp of pain.

——Will you come up here, Kelly, you mesmerized ass, and sit beside your father, roared the figure, half the size of a megalithic cairn. He banged a barrel of a mug on the table, gavelling silence into the din.

——Put an end to your roaring or I'll go down and chew the shrivelled danglers off both of you. Have you no respect for your father?

They had not. Up he jumped on the T-shaped table which heaved under his fatty mass. He heaved himself down to the tangle, buttressed by two screaming women, jumped in the air and landed on their writhing anger. They groaned under the weight. Tarbh, for such was his name, farted down into the mass a stinking, rotted-teeth, acrid smell. He sprang up and down on fat buttocks, pulping peace. Folds of flesh billowed vertically, a contented gash of satisfaction on his elephant sized head. The crushed figures groaned for mercy under his backside.

He removed himself and stood above the squashed figures, unhitched the thongs of his leather breeches, and uncoiled and hosed steaming piss on the groaners. He washed them off the table onto the floor.

The crowd cheered, banging the table with meat bones and oval-headed axes. He turned about massively, like tangled eels in the Saragossa sea, and stalked up the oak boards to his chair.

Kelly's eye fed on the half light and the confusion into which he had been dropped. It was as gruesome as stories about the county home, or the hulks of transit ships.

——Come up here, Kelly, you gawky, double endorsed, watery idiot, with your half-opened gob gaping, as if you were dropped dull.

Kelly stood gummed.

——Do you want me to go down and kick the small arse of you in corduroy trousers, up here.

Kelly pulled his feet out of the muck and started up the whale belly of the low hall.

Outside sounds pinned sea location. A shiver of wind across thatch. Half civil waves springing at stolid rock, reeling back, heaving up, foam tackled, feathered, fluffed, riding in. Kelly grew accustomed to the movement in the half light. A long wide T-shaped table in a T-shaped hut. The T-table planks, glued with decayed food, plates, boat deep, carrying meat and acrid herbs. Sick brown earthen bowls of steaming maze, ladle oars sticky on chipped rims.

——Me only son Kelly, the last of me seed, coming a long journey to see his father, Tarbh roared at the frieze of half finished faces. Kelly, gut cramped with fear, walked up the hall. He stood before Tarbh, terror in his chicken-farm bones. He looked at the debauched head bagged with blue jowls, rotted teeth, breathing poison. Tarbh's tunic and breeches were leather, a thong binding the tunic at the neck, a belt riding on his lard of belly; a codpiece greasy and stained over heavy old balls.

——You are among the immortals, Kelly, the last of them. You are the shakings of the sack and like any son of mine you must go and prove yourself by deed and talk among the mortals. I'm old, Kelly, and soon I'll be taking the boat to the far side, where they have feathered beds and one long easy day. I'll be with the gods beyond the gods beyond the gods. It's a worrying thing managing a field full of unruly whelps of children.

Kelly stood beside him, Mickey O'Gara's poker still in his eye.

——Sit down beside me and tell me this and tell me no more and what were you doing before you got the call back? he asked the pint-sized Kelly. The servant women bundled elk hide on to the chair and put Kelly sitting on it, so that his face peered over the table.

——I was tied to the anvil in Mickey O'Gara's forge, waiting to have a maggot poked out of me eye. He was the biggest, twisted maggot ever seen in the parish, and he would have eaten the soul case out of me if they hadn't cinderised him.

——It's a way, Kelly, we had of getting you back, but you'll lack an eye for the rest of your life, not that it matters. The eye you have will be as good as twenty of the weak and watery ones of the idiots you'll be going back to. It will see the wind and look over the rim of the sky and look into the dodges in men's souls.

Tarbh had a great splutter of talk.

——And Kelly, there is no women in Mayo or the rest of Ireland that it won't charm the heart of, for 'tis an eye that will go flaming red with anger and grow blue in love and black in despair. The cinderated maggot is in your blood and when it has dissolved you won't have a Christian or European thought in the back or the front of your head. We had great unreasonable times before that foreigner, Saint Patrick, came to Ireland. 'Twas a grand life then. Tarbh's name in every mouth, stones to me in every parish in Ireland and, sitting unseen on Tara on autumn sunny days, I would look west towards your miserable County Mayo. And below me, fine fertile land, blue smoky mist and cattle up to their udders in grass, giving more cream than milk. There was milk and honey in the breeze. I was one contented god, deluded in the thought that it would all last forever.

Big tears, the size of oysters, tumbled down Tarbh's face and flopped audibly on oak; rheumy eyes large as small television screens, throwing his memory on to membrane. Kelly twisted his neck out and, screwing his head sideways, could follow the flick, fade and collage of his running thoughts.

—Tell me this Tarbh. Is that Saint Patrick? Kelly asked, pointing to a bishop with his mitre awry, chasing frantic vipers with a crosier out of the mouth of Clew Bay.

—That's him, and that's us there wriggling and writing, for he was a raving terror. He changed it all and wrote about it in a book. We had great times before he came.

Saint Patrick was a man of great fettle, Kelly judged, flailing vipers this way and that with his crook, running here and there until he had them all in the sea and on their way to America. —Hail Glorious Saint Patrick, dear Saint of our Isle, Kelly began with great patriotic fervour, for the maggot ashes hadn't properly dissolved.

—Throw the bugger out, throw the bugger out or I'll stop his holy gob with the knuckles of me fist, a demi-god roared.

—Another word from you, you yob cooted idiot, and I'll powder every bone in your mean carcass into hen dung, Tarbh roared.

Saint Patrick blurred into red anger in Tarbh's eyes. He clawed at the wood of the table, gnashing his gapped teeth.

—Kelly is only learning. Give him time. He's fighting the social conventions of two thousand years. And no bonham ever became a pig in a night, Tarbh told the attentive gods.

Words and anger won. The heckler, who had a crosier mark on his backside, held silence over the mouth of a drink.

—They're a crowd of ignorant idiots. Some of them fellows never went to a school in their lives. The whelps of gods, Kelly, can be a great disappointment. Queer weakness

can show in the strain, like a hidden rot. But it is the infliction of all great men thus to suffer, Tarbh said with nostalgia
for the unborn, but we must be merry men. We'll leave that
to the gods beyond the gods, all of which I strongly doubt,
but we must keep up appearances.

Tarbh looked at the shrivelled size of Kelly beside him.

—You must drink Kelly, for no Celt ever could go across
the sands of a day without wetting his throat. Sober men
have webs about their minds. Reason never answered any
question, and no man was ever reasonable, and it's not inside
in the marrow bone of this race to set out things in clear
lines. I'm no philosopher. They will all come later like carpet-
baggers, pitch their tents inside the minds of men and reduce
them to bone, muscle, testicle and seed. But that's all to
come, Kelly, and you haven't a notion of what I'm going on
about. I'm only a tottering old pagan god, and the smart men
with the books are working against me in Latin, Greek and
High German and they'll chase me out of the woods and
forests into the dark gloomy mountains, where the cold
winds will skin the arse off me.

—God, that's a fair speak from any man, and fair flock
of words are after flying from the culvert of your mouth,
Kelly said.

—'Tis the cycle of things, Kelly. The wooden wheel of
fate turns and creaks and mangles the whole bloody lot of us,
and the hills in the end will be washed away to the sea,
Tarbh said.

—I never looked beyond the hill of tomorrow myself,
Kelly said.

—The Celt, Kelly, is forever looking back and forward,
that's why rushes are growing in half the fields of the country
and him leaning over a stone wall and looking down the road,
waiting for the Sultans of Arabia to pass by, Tarbh told him.

—Declare but I did it myself and a potato drill half dug,
Kelly repented.

—Dreams have kept the belly of the country filled for
four thousand years, Tarbh told him.

—I suppose it's for the same reason that weeds grow in
fields.

—'Tis so, 'tis so, 'tis so, and he let out a long sad osna

and slipped into reverie.

Kelly's eye was again on Tarbh's. A wild track of images ran across his eyes. They jerked and jumped, forests and stumbling little men with tumbling bellies called Bellymen, carrying bulks of clay and stone up mountains' sides to build cairns and forts. They were small and runty like tree butts, whipped on by blond giants. Like all Irishmen in the face of invaders, they were too decent to answer back, but slaved on constructing legends. There were half forests and no forests at all, bounding elks, stones with incised curvilinear decorations, standing stones, stones with small crosses, crosses unobtrusive, among standing stones, then large muscular crosses embossed with images, round towers, Brian Boru on unpolluted Clontarf beach doing his bit. Waterford running with blood and a marriage, then the English more Irish than the Irish, and the Irish, running after the tails of the horses of the nobility, trying to be more English than the English themselves. The disappearance of the gods, industrialisation, and finally reservations for the Irish speaking native population along the west coast.

——You've seen only what the gods see, Kelly. You half understand the vision. The rest of them teething yobs, outside me daughter Maorga, hasn't a clue. But, Kelly, though you weep over what happened and what will happen, I remember when the world was rightly young and a man wasn't tethered to a stake by the chain of mortality or the rope of reason. There is a bit of the Greek in me, lad, more than you might guess and you taking an eye of me. A Greek goddess dropped me on warm sand of a summer night on the western coast. She was tired of that fellow Zeus ordering life on Mount Olympus, so she went and mated with an African. Couldn't satiate her in the high savanna grass. There was pounding and racing and thunder the night I was got, crocodiles crowing, lions roaring and elephants trumpeting out. I was worth the welding and the sweat, for I'm black and white. Dropped on sand like a martin's egg. They were great times. You I have chosen to carry on where I left off. The maggot is an elixir in your blood like ambrosia and nectar. I hear the trumpet out in mid-ocean and when the ship with the flutter of funeral sails comes I'll have to embark for the

Celtic fields in the country of the gods.

Tarbh remembered. His past washed up in his eyes. Kelly saw him before gout bloated his flesh, ague locked his bones. Bacchusbig and bellied he was born, on summer sand from great labour, midwife waves running on the shore. Black afterbirth scooped onto foam and carried seawards as dolphin food. He lived on shell suckle torn from the black rocks, berries, and slept on moss. Flesh of hate and unwanted, quarried in frenzy, dropped on western sand, humped and heavy headed like a court dwarf. Shore abandoned, shorn of the paps, he crawled towards rough food. He never had white child flesh, berry brown and grizzled with salt wind; bowey legged stumble, a man with heavy man's parts and bush of steel coiled hair; right or wrong scotched from his mind. Feed, fill, and rutt as you please.

The repentant mother sent two servant women to search him out among bog and whin and sour rushes, reeds and wind warped woods. Young and sweet like the pink on shells, skin like cream, and blue mediterranean music on their lips.

He led them a race. It was a wild frolic and they grew tired. Dainty dames, wine sippers, undamaged, but their Greek gauze tore on thorned bushes, and they bronzed and hardened. They drank the wash that he had brewed from gutty barley. It was a fine debauch of meat and nuts and berries and wild wash, until they threw away the frayed draperies and the god-girls stood above him hairwild. They danced about him as he gulped from the wine satchel, knawing burnt bones' meat, guffawing laughter at the stars and the small conceits of the gods beyond the gods beyond the gods.

They ripped the dry pelt from him and tossed it in the flame, wash and wind feeding frenzy. He leered like a lord knowing the time ready. They lay and tangled with him, driving him mad, running from him down to the sea. Blind with desire he raved after them. They rolled and tumbled until the dawn. Their laughter ran over the woods, hunting and echoing up among the hills. They gulped the drink and spat it out on his body. They kneaded his belly with kisses, hurting him, maddening him with pleasure. His eyes were corrupt with desire.

Again they ran from him screaming. He pursued them, carrying the satchel of wash in his hand, slugging it, and it ran down his bobbing chops. The smell of their flesh coming on the down wind in his hairy nostrils. He threw the leather bottle from him.

On broken shore bracken and crushed moss the hot mould was cast. A year later here was a litter of lesser gods. They married and mixed in the pot of lust, mating with mother, sister, aunt and grandmother as the fit pushed them, and offsprings came odd, twisted, wanting, wild and wanton, a well-finished god coming in the off-chance.

They were a dark rutty race. Maybe it was the black drop in their blood, the penalty of primitive incest, or the dark, dower clouds siphoning off warm light. Maybe it was a curse or cantankerous genes.

Kelly saw it all run wildly before him, in the big eyes of Tarbh as he dredged up the past from the vaults of his mind.

—That's the way it was, Kelly. That's the way it is. It was arranged like that by others than me and I had no control of what happened. Know this, Kelly, that no man has the shaping of his own life. There is a tangle that unravels itself and we are all the strands. Did you think my first two women fair? Tarbh asked.

—They were grand creatures surely, Tarbh, like a woman I once saw in a carriage from Galway, Kelly told him.

Tarbh laughed, throwing his head back, baying at the beams. He grabbed his barrel of wooden cup in his hands and poured liquor into his gullet. His frame shook, his belly pulsing with liquor.

—Go off with you, Kelly, and he slapped him on the back. Kelly vomited his drink back into his mouth.

—Begod, Kelly, you don't know the havoc age plays on women. There isn't a fair woman born that doesn't turn into a shrivelled hag at fifty. I toss women from me, Kelly, as a boar loses interest in an old sow. They dry up and there is no juice in them. 'Tis a lesson you will learn before the night is out. I will show you something that will blister your mind. Remember, Kelly, you're the last of the gods. After you, there won't be a pagan god left in the world. So you must harden. Love the beautiful women, take them young as you might pluck young flowers, but the spring flower wilts a week after it's cut. Throw it away. Flowers are always springing and the fields are covered with them. But they have only a short stretch and are gone. Be rough and ruthless. Rutt and then away with you.

He banged the table with his mug, stifling the noise of secondary gods.

—Bring in Snua and Grua, he ordered two women who stood near to him. Names once that had soft Greek appellations. I had to paganize them, he told Kelly, do you like the names? he asked then.

—A bit rough and edgy.

—I used to call them Auluinn and Blath. But the names wilted when they grew old.

—But they are bed ridden, a daughter replied.

—Drag the hags in, girl. I want the bold Kelly to see them, and he walloped a daughter onto the floor with his fist, stifling her opinion.

—Trample on women, Kelly. They're a lesser breed. I know their carry on. If you have bedded eight hundred like I have, you get a fair insight to their minds.

—Fair do's to you, Tarbh, Kelly said, the virtue of the maggot now dissolved in his blood.

—Me old flower, Kelly, but you come from decent stock, and he put his arms round Kelly's shoulder and hugged him.

They dragged in Snua by the legs and Grua by the arms, both lamenting about hardhearted daughters.

—They look a thousand years old, Kelly said looking down at the relics.

—Add five hundred more, said Tarbh, and you'll be three hundred out in your answer.

—You don't mean to sit there and tell me that they are a thousand eight hundred years old.

—Correct, me old son of an axe. Them leather old hags have seen eighteen hundred springs, summers, autumns and winters. Did you ever see the like of it in your life?

—They remind me of widow Karragher at home, Kelly slobbered out.

—They were good in their day but they wore out, like the seat of your trousers or the elbows of your shirt. They are dispensable commodities, carrying built-in obsolescence if you will permit a future day expression, Tarbh said.

—You are at liberty to use it, Kelly told him, drunk.

—Thanks, Kelly me old son. I like the bit of independence and anger that is coming into you. And I can see your hair is turning godred like me own.

They looked down at the desiccated mummies.

—They're an offence to my eyes, Kelly told him.

—Take the ugly bitches out of our sight, Tarbh roared, standing up and kicking them on the rumps. They dragged the howling hags from the hall imprecating in high treble.

—You are thinking after me own way Kelly, growing more to me likeness, Tarbh told him.

—I'm on your bloody pagan wavelength. Eat drink and be merry and live to be eight thousand and one, Kelly slobbered out.

—I'll drink a pot of drink to that.

And he held out his wooden tumbler for more. He slugged, Kelly slugged. He slugged, Kelly slugged. He slugged, Kelly slugged. They threw the mugs on the floor and danced them to pulp. They climbed on to the table and started dancing to the skirl of a bagpipes made from pigs' bladders.

The crowd of lesser gods who held great places on the tongues of the old storytellers, stood about the platform of the table and cheered. They knocked their mugs together and toasted the health of the young god. They fought among themselves, spat, cursed, smashed at each other's heads. They trampled a dwarf into mash on the floor.

It was a great night by their standards, one not to be forgotten when they got to telling their stories.

CHAPTER THREE

The Halligans had standing among the tinkers of Connaught. Their line stretched back further than their stories could remember, and they flattered themselves with the notion that somewhere in the tangle of their history one of them had been induced into a royal bed to replenish weak stock and kill a recurring curse of beautiful idiots.

One of the women had been got in a tavern by a rakish prince from England who left her with a litter of twin males. When the males grew to stature it was said that they bore the resemblance of a man on an old coin. Great play was made of the resemblance and their status rose until they became the royalty among the tinkers of Connaught.

Their movements were as regular as the Church Calendar. They set their lives by Old Moore's Almanac. They went from fair to fair, and were known in the market place of every town at gymkhanas, strand races, patterns, and periodic apparitions. They spent their winters in Galway, and their summers in north Mayo and Sligo.

They were in the horse, goat and white she-ass business, and there was not a known defect in a horse which they did not recognise instantly. Their horses were sold to the British army and shipped off to wars on the confines of the empire. One of these geldings had a decoration from Queen Victoria. Their goats were sold to the coal mines of Wales where, blind, they pulled trollies of coal through labyrinths to feed the industrial Minotaur. Their white she-asses went to Algiers and their milk was used in the baths of Pasha Harin's harem to keep his women buttocky and white. They exported the white she-asses through Galway port, and they went south in a ship tackled with silk.

Power had absolutely corrupted them, for neither the forces of church or state could tether them under any law. Birth, terminal disease and marriage were blessed by the Church but outside that they had not much trucking with religion. They never paid oats money, attended a station or dropped a copper in a collection box at a church door. Peelers held them in awe. Here were men they feared to tackle with gun or truncheon. Many a peeler was less an eye or a tooth or an ear for his arrogance in tangling with them. Magistrates feared their tempers ever since Justice Brown was waylaid on a lonely road and tied naked to an ass's back. The whole night he had been carried through bog and small road and in the morning the ass with Justice Brown strapped to his back was found grazing on the Mall in Castlebar. No evidence could be laid against them since it was a dark night and the Justice was the only witness.

They were fierce men in any struggle or fight. They would start a mêlée on a Saturday evening to make a dark night interesting. They were worst of all when they turned on themselves. Fighting was a fever in their blood. They raked up differences and insults until the small towns echoed with the fury of their blows and the curses of their tongues.

Their leader was Angel Halligan. He had a mind as mild as milk. A middle-size man with no outstanding attribute except a broken, angular nose. He was married to Delia Cuff, a strutter of a woman, with a hugh splay of backside, unkempt black hair, gapped teeth. She had a raucous voice and every time she opened her mouth she minted a new simile or metaphor. Between her floppy dugs nestled her clay pipe on grocershop string. In a contemplative mood she suckled the pipe over a turf fire or, leaning against a warm bank of summer moss, her mind masticated experience. Periodically she would put a full stop to her thoughts with a jet of brown saliva. She was a size and a half larger than experience and her knickers was made from two white flour bags. Later when farmers wanted to express the unnatural size of a calf or a bonham they would say, ——She was half the size of big Delia Cuff's knickers and that says something for the animal.

In a temper, she was like the whole world up in anger, panting, raging, hoarse. She kicked skillet pots off fires, blistering every man of the tribe with a turbulence of bitter words. She balanced out all the wants in Angel Halligan.

She was the mother of ten and not one girl among the brood. They were all like herself in their anger. The eldest of them was called Foxy Halligan, with hair as red as rusty iron. A huge, ugly, mean-eyed giant, he could lift an ass under his elbow, or pull a cow out of a bog hole by the tail. A morose brooder, he hated everybody, and anger smouldered in the ashes of his eyes, until the breath of a fight stirred it to flame. He was no company for civil men, though he had a good eye for a horse and could smell rusty scrap iron a mile off. When his father's bones were under clay he would take the leadership of the tribe.

They were on their way into Balla from Claremorris. It was a day in July with green optimism growing in the fields. The light wind tumbled lightly on barley and hay and came ashore on the ditches. There was stir of activity on the road, as mean, thin cattle headed west to Balla fair. Farmers eyed the byroads where cattle might turn left or right, and periodically dart with windmill hands to turn them off as soon as they saw danger. Pigs grunted in creeled carts; there was an ass or two on the road, a cart carrying a man or his wife, quiet as the slow clouds.

—If any man sees a white she-ass within braying distance of Balla buy him, for your man from Algiers will be dropping his anchor in Galway come July, Foxy Halligan had told the tribe and them gathered around the night fires. Pay anything up to fifty pounds for her or our luck with the east will run out.

—But there isn't a white she-ass left between here and Clifden. If there was we would have smelt its milk on the wind, Big Delia Cuff told him.

—Stop your gob, woman, but there are places in these parts from where men haven't stirred for the last hundred years thinking that Cromwell is ravaging the land. Maybe there are acres of white she-asses if a man had his ear to the wind, Foxy told her.

—Search where you will, but by the cheeks of me backside you won't find them, she replied.

—It's only saying it, I am. Be on the look out and if you see one put your fist in your pocket and pay fifty pounds and bring it to the camp, Foxy told them.

The wind scratched the soft bellies of clouds and carried them east. Yet, with his sure eye to the vagaries of the sky, Foxy knew that there might be rain in the evening. They went down the road to Balla with their coloured caravans, their carts and tents, their piebald horses and retinue of fiery eyed goats. Farmers looked at them as they passed by. The Halligans were as proud as landed families, and a man would do bad to cross them in an argument or bargain. They were known the length and breadth of the county for their fast angers, their cudgels and fists. So farmers held their silence and kept their bitter words to themselves or for quiet bed talk when a man could speak out his feelings against the world.

They moved into the crotch of Balla. It was a day of movement, knotted with hard-faced men conspiring to buy and sell. Cowdung smaddered on to the cobblestones and was carried by wellingtons down the road and into bars. The smell stood ten feet high and had the width and breadth of the town. Here and there stalls yawned with rows of army coats, heavy boots, horse tackle, rope, cheap and genuine. Meat stalls bled. June midges buzzed and swarmed, hard and purple. Fresh fish from Belmullet, lined lifeless with startled eyes; cocks of carrageen moss and purple dilsk with pendant barnacles reeked of the sea. Jobbers from Mullingar, foreign as Phoenician sailors, flayed pound notes from thick wads sealing bargains with spits.

In the far corner of the market stood Pike Fogarty the Balladeer singing a song about Kate Houlihan. He croaked out the words to an indifferent audience and a rash of tinker children.

> Come all you lads and lassies
> And listen to my song
> Of beautiful Kate Houlihan
> I won't detain you long.
> There never was a creature

Since God created Eve
Of beauty and distinction
To make a fine man grieve.
She stands above the Corrib Lake
Her skin is like the dawn,
A man would walk a thousand miles
To see this Cailín Bán.
If I were king of England
Or skipper of his ships,
I'd give the treasure that I own
To kiss her crimson lips.

It went on for eighty verses, long and tedious as a road through a bog. His Adam's apple agitated with emotion as he scraped music beneath the words, complaining that he would wander the roads of Ireland tormented with the thought of Kate. An indifferent wind carried the music into the middle of the square where it was trampled on by heavy boots. He thought to himself that they were a hard-hearted lot and that there was no tune which could strike water from the rocks of their souls.

Caoc Ainsworth sat in Rafferty's shebeen mulling over the generalities of a fair day, and a fast way of turning an opportunity into gold coins. He had dodgy eyes, a sailor's gait, and he could never get out of his mind the fact that the world wasn't a rolling ship. He waddled when he walked. He had knowledge of all the seas. He had rounded all capes and followed the white whales of the Indian Ocean. He had a black wife and a brown son on a foreign island, he said, where coconuts fell into the sea and were swept up to Arabia. A man could come twenty times in a night if he suckled their milk. Suckle them he must have, for he was worn to a thread.

In through the door of Rafferty's shebeen came Casta, the Halligan idiot, with a foolish, slobbery gob on him. He was the gliogar egg in the nest, and had hatched out into a fool. His hunger and thirst were endless and if heaven was bacon and porter and cauldrons of spuds, he wanted to go there. He pounded on the counter and the sight of him brought the barman running.

—A plate of bacon and spuds and two pints of porter

and where is the back? he asked. It was a rote phrase with him. When the plate of bacon and spuds was laid before him and the pint glass in his hand he asked the barman, ——You didn't hear of a braying white she-ass in these parts, be any chance, for me brother Foxy is willing to put fifty pounds in the hand of any man who can lead him to such a miracle of an ass.

——Faith, sure the last white she-ass around these parts ate grass over in Knocksoxon, ten years ago. No, there are none of them left, the barman told him.

——'Tis a great pity now and the man from Africa coming in his boat to buy them.

Caoc Ainsworth listened. If there was gold to be made it could be made here, but he would have to take to his heels after he had finished his bargaining. He walked over to Casta Halligan.

——You were talking of white asses, he said.

——I was. But the place is bled dry of every one of them, he moaned.

——Now maybe it is and maybe it isn't if a man threw his eye in the right direction. I'd be thinking myself that the only two white she-asses belonging to anyone, belong to myself, but I have them in a shed outside the town as they don't take kindly to the sun, Caoc Ainsworth said confidentially.

——White asses? Casta Halligan asked.

——As white as the down on a goose, or snow in winter, or candles burning in the church.

——I'd like to see them asses, Casta Halligan said.

——Well I never let them out into a field until the dark is falling, for as I say the sun would turn them to yellow and no one wants to buy yellow ass, Caoc Ainsworth told him.

——No, there is no market for yellow asses, Casta Halligan agreed.

——That's why I keep them away from the sun, for white mushrooms only grow at night, Caoc continued.

——You wouldn't be thinking of parting with them? Casta asked.

——Well I would, though with great reluctance because them asses mean more to me than the women of Bangalore, but I'm going to Belmullet to board a boat for China and leave them I must.

——I'd give a cart of bonhams to see them.

——See them you will and the sun setting. But you and no one else for I've taken to your ways and any one I take to, me asses take to also, for being white they have queer peculiarities.

——I once knew a man who could talk to a sheep dog which would do anything that he said.

——There, what did I say?

——And I once went to a circus where a horse could count better than myself.

——There is no end to wonders. Now if you wait for me outside Doran's pub this evening, I'll take you to where the asses graze, but have the money and two sheets to cover the asses because even a yellow moon might turn their colour, Caoc told him.

——I'll be there. But be all that's held holy, if the asses aren't there I'll hang you with a halter from a hawthorn bush, Casta swore.

When the bargain was made, Caoc winked at Casta and went off to the hardware shop. He bought a bucket of white-wash and went south out of the town to Martin Costello's field. He mixed the whitewash thick and gave the two grey asses an undercoat. He ran them around the field six or seven times until they were dry. Then he put on two overcoats until the braying asses were like celestial animals careering across the pastures of heaven. There was no knowing what trouble he was calling down on his head, he thought, but if he got the money, he would take to the sea again and sail off to the islands or the eastern ports. No Halligan ever went far in a boat and no horse ever raced across the waves other than the horse of the old god.

The evening smouldered, and sulky clouds, afflicted with gouty rain stood beyond the hills.

——If it rains, I'll spend the night hanging from a black-thorn tree with a tinker's rope around me neck, Caoc Ainsworth said to himself, but the temptation of ports and the smiling teeth of matey women was too much for him.

Caoc Ainsworth walked down the main deck of the town.

He looked at the spreading sail of cloud, the tree tackle above the town. He smelt rain on the wind. It would be a good night to weigh anchor and set out from the introspective harbour of Westport. There were dawns in the east to brighten his eyes and coral sands flecked with silver which would suck the dampness out of his bones.

The swarm of noises above and about the market, like the flapping wings of irresolute crows, came home to brood in small knots of men. Cattle, tired and stale, stood brooding, lacking confidence. Splattered dung, boot marked, stiffened and died. Gaudy stalls folded. Here and there stood islands of potatoes, creels or sally rods. Evening thickened on the square like a lament for the dead.

Casta Halligan, weighed down with gold and his mind on white asses, had his backside to the wall of Doran's pub. His trousers were never so heavy before in his life. There would be high praise for him when he walked down the street of Balla towing two asses. He would sit and tell everyone how it happened. Already he had his beginning line.

—I was within in Rafferty's shebeen saying nothing and sitting over me potatoes and porter, when this fellow about the size of Angel came over to me. I eyed him and he eyed me. He said to me in a slow voice, —I heard you talking about white asses. —You did, said I.

This was as far as he had got in his story, but it would grow and he would put a good tail to it.

—Did you bring the money? Caoc Ainsworth asked when they met.

—I did, and he rattled the evidence in his pocket.

—And the sheets for accoutring the donkeys, that they will not be blemished with moonlight?

—Here they are under me elbow and in a sack, that no one might be curious about me intentions.

—Well pretend that you have no interest in anything in particular and everything in general. Walk circuitous, for there are eyes behind every window, Caoc said.

—Sure I know. Haven't walls eyes and you can't say a thing that isn't heard, Casta replied.

They got up on Caoc's pacer of a mare, cropping a triangular patch of grass where the roads came together, and headed in the direction of Costello's field. When Casta saw the two white she-asses in the centre of the field, his mouth opened like a gate letting cattle in.

—If you must look at them, look at them by the light of holy candles and sprinkle them with holy water, Caoc Ainsworth said.

They covered the asses with sheets, struck the bargain and went their different roads. Caoc jumped on his horse and rode across country towards Westport. Casta, proud as a prince, led the two whitewashed asses back along the road to Balla. Still holding the long reins, he went into Ned Muldoon's pub and called to Foxy, —Foxy, I have something out in the footpath here that will bring the light into your eye.

—Not a white ass?

—No, but two of them.

—You better be sure no one has pulled wool over your eyes or I'll eat you without salt.

—As sure as I'm standing here but the likes of them for whiteness never was seen since snow began to fall.

They went out onto the street and looked at the braying sheets.

—It could be the funeral of two ghosts from what I can make out. What are the sheets doing over them? Foxy asked and went to draw them away.

—Don't, Foxy, not in the light. If a thin bent ray of light fell on them, they'd turn yellow.

—Blast, man, if you can't see them in the light, you'll never see them at all.

—Only be Church candles can they be seen, the man said. Because the light has the Pope's blessing, it doesn't turn white asses yellow.

A crowd drained from the pub, poulticed out by interest. They tethered attention to Foxy and Casta Halligan and let it graze. With the talk of the Pope and blessed candles and Caoc Ainsworth laying down intricate canons about the colour balance of asses, they knew there was a hoax somewhere. Caoc was the great deceiver. He had robbed widows of their earnings, left others carrying duplicate twins with a promise of marriage and stolen the slates off Tobar chapel when the parish priest was away at Lisdoonvarna.

—I know nothing about these queer rites. They are strange conditions but I'll abide be them, ever since I saw statues bleed in Leitrim, Foxy Halligan said.

The crowd followed the braying asses down the town to the church. Father Green heard the noise in the presbytery but gave it no account.

—You'll have to get Father Green to open the Church and it's only death that will get him out at night, an old lady told Foxy.

—We'll see, we'll see, Foxy said.

He went through the small graveyard and up to the presbytery. He thundered at the door. A timid, looped little woman with a thin beard on her chin came out and looked up at him.

—Is the priest at home? he asked.

—The priest's at home boy and may not be seen, she said.

—It's not very easy speaking to Father Green, he told her.

—No, you wait till I go and see, the holy father is drinking his tea, she said.

—Cut out talking in ballad rhymes and tell him to come out here on the double and tell him that Foxy Halligan said so.

—Is it Foxy Halligan the Tinker?

—Yes, Foxy roared at her.

—Oh, ocon, she cried and skittered away like a frightened mouse.

Father Green came to the door in a snuffy soutane. He carried silver rimmed reading glasses on the bridge of his nose and looked over them at Foxy.

—What in the name of God can I do for you at this hour of night. Is one of you dying up in the market square?

—No, sir, but I want a bundle of candles blessed be the Pope and a can of holy water, Foxy said directly.

—And what would any Christian be wanting with them at this hour of the night? Father Green asked.

—I want to take a look at two white asses that a brother of mine has bought from some fellow with squinty eyes, he told the priest.

Father Green had read history and knew the cause of wars. Knowing that ignorance is a common commodity, he opened the church door and brought out a bundle of unblessed candles and a bucket of secular water.

—Are they blessed by the Pope? Foxy Halligan asked.

—Indeed they are and I have certificates to prove it, Father Green told him.

—Is there enough water there to perform a miracle? Foxy asked.

—No, you need eight barrels for a miracle but there is enough here to keep asses out of harm's way.

—What do I owe you for the candles and water? Foxy asked.

—Three pounds and you are getting a good bargain.

Foxy stopped by a coffee-table tombstone and by candle-light laid out three dirty pounds on incised lettering.

—There you are father. It's you that has the power, he told Father Green.

Half the town was in the graveyard, standing on slabs and bumps of clay or straddled on the arms of Celtic crosses.

—What in God's name is after happening? somebody asked at the rim of the crowd.

—Foxy Halligan is after seeing an apparition. He's gone over to Father Green to make a confession.

—That will take him a year.

—And he's going off then to Roscrea.

—Wonders will never cease.

—Who did he see?

—They don't know whither it is Saint Patrick or Saint Joseph, but who ever he saw told him that if he didn't repent his ways, maggots would eat him before the year was out.

—His hand is being forced.

Speculation was rampant on the dark road. About the two animals candles were lighting brightly, casting religious light on the sheeted asses.

—Ready now with the bucket of holy water, when I pull the sheets away? Foxy directed. —Now, and he whipped the sheets off the asses' backs. True enough they were as white as leprosy. There were never two white asses like them in the annals of any ass race. When Pike Fogarty

saw them, rhymes started barking in his head. Casta poured
the water over their back, slowly intoning ——amen, amen,
amen.

The two asses brayed out over the silence. The sacredness
dripped from them in small drops of whitewash.

——Give me a candle for a minute, Foxy said, but I think
that we have been outdone by some tangler or other.

He went over to one of the sacred asses and rubbed her
hump. Whitewash came off in his palm. He tore at the white
coats. Shreds of stiff whitewash fell away.

——They're only whitewashed asses. We've been done, I'll
hang some crosseyed bastard for this from the rafter of his
kitchen. Come here, Casta, he ordered.

——Easy now, Foxy, don't lose your head. How was I to
know they were whitewashed. Sure only the devil in hell
would think of a plan like that, Casta said in defence.

The light of two candles was spluttering in Foxy's mad
eyes.

——Who is he and where did he go?

——I don't know his name, Foxy, but he's a dry faced
sailor now on his way to Belmullet to board a ship to China,
he cried.

Foxy hit him a clout on the ear.

——Don't hit me, Foxy. Don't, he cried.

——How much did you give him? Foxy asked.

——A hundred pounds, he told Foxy.

——And who gave it to you? Foxy asked.

——I took it out of the mattress in your caravan. Sure you
told us to buy any white ass within braying distance of Balla,
Casta said.

——Who was he and I'll tear his nuts out? Foxy roared.

——A little bent man, with bowey legs, and a squint in his
eye, Casta said.

——It's Caoc Ainsworth, the great deceiver sure enough,
and even you, Foxy Halligan, won't catch him, for he's as
slippery as an eel, Terence Wade, a low class tinker, said.

There was malice and delight in his eye. Foxy Halligan
tore at his throat.

——Laugh at a man's misfortune will you? and he viced
Wade's throat with hard fingers. But the Wades had kept

close to one another. A blackthorn knob drew blood from Foxy Halligan's scalp. The war was on. It was a quiet night and candles burned grimly on grave slabs. They threw soft cloister light on the fighting. It moved one way and then another across the graveyard. Railings were savaged from the earth and turned into spears. Some took refuge under tombstones and feigned dead. Others ran from the graveyard and made their way across the fields. Three hours it lasted. Then there was peace and Foxy ordered the camp to break and move towards Belmullet.

It was a good night for sailing out across Clew Bay. Caoc passed the hump back of Clare Island, huddled up for the night, rain caressing its rump. He named the stars of the east to himself, and thought of the thighs of black women under coconut trees.

CHAPTER FOUR

—It's me daughter Maorga, Tarbh said looking down the hall.

His daughter stood framed in the doorway, scrawny, like a starved crane. A tusky yellow buck tooth clamped her underlip. Eunuch whiskers, countable, grew on the ledge of a gubbed chin. Around her narrow shoulders she wore a purple cloak secured by a bronze pin. Her hair, rope ravelled, was creasote brown. Kelly had laid his eyes on wake hags, but she was uglier than them all.

She made her way up the hall, clawed at, as she hobbled on her lame step. Kelly had never seen such a desiccated face before. She took a seat beside her father, grunted at him, then ladled porridge into her mouth with her fingers. She wiped the slobber from her face and drank dark wine from a mug.

—Who's he? she asked, looking at Kelly.

—He's a relation called Kelly from Mayo.

—We have no relations called Kelly.

—We have in Mayo.

—Well I never heard of them. How did you get that black hole in your eye, you runt?

—A fellow by the name of Mickey O Gara, a blacksmith in our parish, did it on a fair day, exorcising a maggot.

—He should have thrown you in the fire and reddened iron with you.

Kelly disliked the insult.

—I'll take a hawthorn stick to you. I'm not here to be insulted by a black hag and don't insult Mayo, for it's a place of outstanding people.

—You're not worth a damn the whole lot of you.

Anger flooded through Kelly.

—Let me at her. Let me at her with a blackthorn stick. I'll leave memorable marks on her.

Still not god-size, he stood on his chair and stretched across at her. They would have torn at one another's throats had not Tarbh pushed them back.

—Don't think that my father, the drunken woman walloper, has given you licence to savage women with his raimeis. Big though you'll be, a woman will soften the brutality in you some day, you skut of a Mayo man.

Kelly was up again, god larger now, for he grew like a mushroom, by the minute.

—I'll knock ropes of tar out of you, he cried.

—Enough of noise, Tarbh roared, my head is bursting with bad drink. I want a story.

There might have been more fighting had not a figure made his appearance at the door.

—Did you save Ireland? Tarbh called down to him.

—I did but it took me all me time. There is no doubt, but the men going now aren't half the men they were. A blow of a nettle would knock them down.

—What was the weather like? Tarbh said.

—It was bad down at Sliabh Lucra but there's a grand sun out at Howth with all the Fianna lying out on the sand reciting poetry and healing their wounds and getting a nice colour up for the women in winter. Others were learning how to pick thorns out of their heels and them running.

—How was Mac Cumhail?

—Complaining bitterly about everything. He has ague in his bones and drinks nothing but milk, for his stomach is coming against him.

—Not half the man he was.

—About an eighth, he replied.

—Time to retire to the bit of land we have staked out for ourselves in the land of the dead.

—Have you a story for us? Tarbh asked.

—Indeed I have, if I could put something inside me leather skirt, and the throat is at me for I knocked up queer mileage between Cork and Dublin.

——Come up to the head of the table, take your ease for a while and when the humour is on you, take the weight of time off our minds by the talk of your adventures.

——This is The Bodach of the Patched Coat, Tarbh told Kelly.

——I've heard of him and his great story, Kelly said.

——Put it there, said the Bodach, stretching out his hand, stained with wet blackberry mash. He was as thin as a long rake, give or take an inch. He had an Adam's apple of a hump. The hump slipped up and down his back when he panted, as if it were a frightened rabbit. There was barely enough skin to stretch from bone to bone. The skin in general was a size too small for the bone work, and Kelly thought it might snap under the strain. His head was like his back bone, narrow as a nail, and nose, eyes, ears and chin were cast in the same proportion.

He poured a drink down his throat. Kelly could hear it run down the slope of his water tube and into the pool of his stomach. The drought killed, he began.

——If there is one thing I can't stand, under the light of heaven, it's arrogance.

——That's not the way to begin, someone called, tell us the story as it happened. Never mind off-limit comments.

——It was a right morning, the Bodach said, the day throwing the slitter of sun into a porridge bowl of sky, like the yoke in the white of the egg. Firm and bright it stood, giving radiance and health to the Five Provinces of Ireland, the Isle of Man and Achill. The bees were busy, mumbling between the flowers gathering honey. Blackbirds were singing in the valleys by the sound of women-murmuring streams.

——That's the old style, a listener called.

——Don't interrupt me and knock me off key and me getting the hum of me consonants right, the Bodach of the Patched Cloak said. Ireland was white under the sun when the heavy-snoring, light-hearted, winter-weary Fianna went up the cliffs of Beann Eadair to flip open their tents of trousers and have their morning slash off the cliffs and sniff in the nine o'clock breeze.

——Slop, somebody interrupted, you can't be introducing low incidents like that. Leave them noble with their pure hearts and light thoughts.

——I can only report what I saw, the Bodach said, but what they saw was a wonderous ship sailing towards the coast of Ireland. Lacing up their trousers, they ran from the wine-dark sea down to where Finn was drawing on his boots over gouty legs. They told him of the tall ship coming towards Ireland, with tall silk sails and a warrior of great stature standing like a German statue in the front deck. As the sea smelt of salt, and a mountain of heather, so this smelt of danger to Ireland.

The keel grated on the shore and this chap jumped out where the Fianna had gathered with their mouths opened, for he was accoutred in gold armour, fine leather, white silk, the likes of which had not been seen in the country before. Finn, puffing out his chest, bellied down to the shore and without any informalities, said, ——Who the hell are you and what are you doing trespassing on these shores without right or warrant. Be off with you where you came from.

——So this is the traditional graciousness of Ireland, said the prince fellow, haughty as you like.

——I don't like the look of your gob or the cultured sound of your voice, Finn said, you remind me too much of traditional enemies.

——I presume you are Finn Mac Kool.

——You presume right and who might you be with your smart talk and the superiority of a tourist.

——I am from Thessolonica, and I come to challenge your best runners in a race. If I am victor I shall claim yearly levies of gold and cattle from this island.

——Thessolonica! Thessolonica? muttered the Fianna, not very strong in geography.

——So you're a runner and judging by the shape of you, you wouldn't last a half-mile with the worst of us, Finn told him.

——I challenge your best runner in a race, from, he took a map out of his pocket and studied it, from Sliabh Luchra in Cork to Howth.

——Seeing that we have nothing to do for the next month

or two it might prove entertainment for us, Finn told him.

Finn looked round at the berry-brown, deer-fast, noble minded soldiers with an eye to picking out the best of them, when from nowhere I strayed down the hill towards them, with my ground-long, multicoloured, patched, thorn torn cloak and the look of a yob on me gob. I picked a few daisies and made them into a chain and put them on my head. I took a bone from a pouch and gnawed it. It got great attention.

—Excuse me a minute, I said, but I heard great talk of running. Well I'm a bit of a champion meself and I lay a challenge at the feet of the man from strange parts.

The sky rang with laughter. Some fell in contortions on the ground writhing, others cooped their sides with their hands. I let them have their sport and eat me pig-sweet Tara-reared bone. I gave Finn a hard stare with me magical eyes and knew that I had won me place in the race. He sucked his burnt thumb and knew that Ireland was in serious danger and me the man of the moment.

—Right, he said, we'll give you the chance to prove your talk. I'll hand over the salvation of the country to you.

So down through the country we went, by different ways and pitched camps on Sliabh Luchra. He had grand furnishings surely. A tent, eight-sided, with flags fluttering. Inside was a bed of swan down and outside he had hung his silk underwear. It was like the cloud palace that you would see in the sky of a summer day. He was washing his teeth before retiring when I went over to him and asked would he come hunting. But no. He never slept with meat in his stomach. So off I went and speared a boar, spitted him over a fire and eat him and lowered a barrel of drink. I sowed some of the patches of me cloak, made a tent from it and slept.

—Time to begin the race, he said early in the morning.

—Off you go, said I, but I have only got half my sleep.

He started off in great style and back I went to bed. The sun was half way up the sky when I started from me breakfast, having wrapped some of the left-overs in me cloak in case hunger would strike me down on the way. I passed him at Cashel, his fine skin pouring out sweat, his Greek nostrils sucking in air. At Portarlington I sat and eat the rest of my bones, and lay in a warm ditch waiting for him.

—You left half your cloak on a hawthorn bush thirty miles back, he said, running by me and me milking the tits of the noon day sun. He was telling the truth. I felt half dressed, so back I went and retrieved it, and then on after him, hell for leather. I was sitting at Blessington eating me mash of blackberries and oats when he came past again saying I had left me satchel of bones fifty miles back. And so I had. So I balled the mash into the tail of me cloak and back I went.

On Howth the Fianna were palpitating with anxiety. They looked at the Wicklow Hills and saw the prince making great headway and me not within roaring distance of him. They sent up a great cry and grieved that Ireland was lost to the invader. On he came by Clontarf strand, puffing and blowing, his face blue with effort. And then down from the Dublin hills I streaked after the manner of the wind and passed him within fifty yards of the running post. The Fianna sent a great cry into the sky and said Ireland was saved. I sat on a tuft of grass and started eating me interrupted mash, when along came the prince in fury. He had his sword out and he would have gone through them like a whale through a shoal of herrings or a hawk through a flock of starlings, but I rolled the berries and meal into a hard ball and flung it in his direction. Declare but I knocked his head the wrong way round. We made him promise to send a tribute of gold and soap every year to Ireland, set him on board the ship and sent him on his way. In this manner and there isn't a word of a lie in the story, for I told it as it happened without adding or taking from it, Ireland was saved. There was great wonderment and talk as they stood on the sea-worn, foot-trampled sand. So I slipped back over the hill and came home.

There was a pause in the hall, every mouth hanging loose following the running feet of the words. There had been many great stories told in the hall, but this outclassed the whole lot of them and they said that it would last for ever in men's minds.

Kelly had heard it before from a passing fiddler in his own home. There had been bits added to it and bits taken from it. Worst of all the fiddler was an atheist and said he didn't believe half the talk that went on about the gods but it was a way he had of earning a few coppers. Kelly now knew that it was a true story.

He sat at the top of the table and he noticed that a magical sleep was falling on the dark hut. The gods beneath him were falling across the table, snoring gently, the torches, guttering, were trailing dead, black smoke, the hungry dogs had collapsed on their paws. The bulk of Tarbh keeled over and began snoring. When he snored in, the walls and roof drew in in sympathy. When he snored out, they bulked out. A fog of sleep was drifting in across the sea of Kelly's mind. The hall darkened and he fell forward.

CHAPTER FIVE

Mad Houlihan was a mystery. There was no knowing where
he came from. He sailed into the Corrib from Galway one
summer's evening across the silk of the lake, his eyes burning
with madness. He looked at the shape and contour of the
land, silent and contemplative, the sailors pulling their oars
through slack water with soft strokes.

He staked out a hundred acres of land between middle
mountain and sea. Then he began to build his castle. The
shape of the castle followed the mad order of his mind. It
was a mongrel of stone, set in a kennel of high wall which
bounded the land he had bought. Its mad architecture was
drawn from all the strange lands which he had ever visited.
Doric columns carrying a pediment containing the Flight of
the Wild Geese from Limerick fronted the house. An Italian
portico ran east and west from the main building, where he
could walk during the thin warmth of summer. The
rectangular castle looked onto geometric French gardens with
small neat hedges. In the centre a fountain sprang into the
air, spread out symmetrically and fell onto tiers of marble
basins. An onion-shaped dome stood at the north corner, a
minaret in the shape of the Vimana of Tanjore in the west.
In the south a spire of a gothic cathedral. In this manner he
placated all the gods of his mind.

Year after year, barges carried the art treasure of the world
up through the tunnelled canal which led to a small harbour
in the castle. There were Gallo-Roman bronze bowls, ivory
jars with pierced panels, ewers engraved and inlaid, mosaics
from Ravenna, jugs in copper with repoussé decorations,

paintings on silk from China, folding screens from Japan,
jade vessels, manuscripts, musical instruments, rare manuscripts from Italy, furniture from Spain. Each object was
placed in its proper room, and each room was hung with its
proper tapestry, scroll or painting.

Beyond the house in the wide gardens, he ran paths among
rare trees, built grottoes, Japanese pagodas, gazeboes and set
rare shrubs and plants. Here was the learning of the whole
world.

At night the lake was often disturbed by the roar of lions,
the jibber of monkeys, the trumpeting sound of elephants,
the chatter of paroquets carried to the gardens. There was no
doubt in men's mind that he was mad. Being poor and mad
meant that man carried distortions in his imagination. Being
rich and mad meant that the distortions received shape and
brooded over the small market village of Pool Dubh. The
villagers wondered who he was and where he had come from.
And they asked one another if it were true that there were
dungeons of gold under the castle. He had half a thousand
servants working within the walls, black men and brown men,
yellow men, and queer featured men from the middle of
Russia.

Mad Houlihan was a distortion. He carried a huge hump on
his back that weighed him into the ground. His right foot
which he dragged after him was short and clubbed. The head
on no neck was outsized and carried a huge brain which never
slept.

He started life as a sailor. He undertook dangerous
journeys through southern seas and collected enough money
to buy a ship of his own. He knew the markets. What was
rare was wonderful, and what was wonderful brought in large
profits. And he knew also that what was rare in the west
was common in the east, what was rare in the east was
common in the west. So he carried spice from India to New
York, and baubles from New York to India. He shipped silk
from Japan and returned with calico. Within three years he
had two ships, within five, eight, and after ten he was the
master of a large fleet. So gold poured through his hands and
he satiated every twisted taste he ever had.

Being Irish he never forgot two things. The first was that

the history of Ireland was sad enough to make any good man weep. A fiddler and harper always travelled with him, played to him and reminded him of the glory and misery of the race. The more he heard the haunting songs and his ship harboured in Morocco, Buenos Aires, Calcutta or Shanghai, the more he thought of restoring Ireland to its place among the races of the world. The second was that Ireland was formerly a land of saints and scholars. He was a religious maniac. He became a student of comparative religions. For six months of every year he went on pilgrimage to some sacred shrine or other. In this way he visited the temples of India, the shrines of Russia, the Kaaba of Mecca. He talked with holy men here, there and everywhere and he could quote every sacred book ever written. He had ikons, statues, prayer-wheels, incense burners, candlesticks, illuminated manuscripts in every corner of his ship. It was whilst travelling in Austria that he discovered his true vocation, that of restoring the Irish race to its true stature among the peoples of the world. He saw a way of elevating it above the second-rate degenerate races and cleansing it of contamination. It would be possible to produce a race clear and fresh as well-water. There were too many half-finished failures in the world. And it all happened in a monastery garden. One Austrian evening he was walking through religious paths thinking of nothing in particular when he saw a priest nosing his way through a pea garden. They were peculiar types of peas in that at one end of the plot they were small and runty, at the other tall and aristocratic and in between normal enough for that time of year. The priest held a large magnifying glass to his eye and went slowly from pea to pea, chuckling with innocent delight.

—Tell me now father, he said, going over to the insignificant figure, why do your peas give you such delight?

—What's that, what's that? the priest asked absentmindedly.

—You get great pleasure from looking at garden peas, Mad Houlihan said.

—Ah, ah, but they are more than garden peas. You are looking at the very secrets of the world here. Locked inside these walls is more knowledge than you'll find in any book, he told Mad Houlihan.

So Houlihan heard him out. The priest explained about selection, and told him that he could predict what he could expect when he crossed certain strains of plants. That not only could a man, if he desired, improve the strain of plants, but also of animals and men. It was all very difficult in the case of men because it was almost impossible to trace the traits that went to the making of any human being. But all Houlihan needed was the wind of the word.

He sweated a whole night deep in thought. If only he could lay his hands on the perfectly unspoiled Celt and mate it with the best blood in the continent of Europe, he could produce a race the likes of which never raised its eyes to a morning sun or put its hand to a plough.

Now his life found some purpose. He sailed to Galway city and travelled up the Corrib until he found a hundred acres of land facing south, like a large window. He threw up a ten foot wall about it, built a castle to his own dreams, crammed it with treasures and filled the library with every annal, book and record kept in Ireland for the last thousand years. Then he locked himself in the castle for two years and when he emerged he knew he had discovered the only two true Celts left in the country. The wise men, the ballad men, the old men with long memories had come to help him. They talked, and wondered, looked up place names, followed small migrations, checked shipping lists, tombstone inscriptions, church records. Then they drew out large, tangled family trees on a blackboard, transferred them to paper until finally all the roots, trunk, and branches fell into place.

In May he started in search of the Carney family. He wandered from village to village, bedded down in small hotels and questioned the travelling people of the roads, the tinkers, the parish priests. Finally he found the Carneys in a small twisted street of stooped houses in a large town in Louth. It was a tradesman's street, full of artisan activity. Sign boards stood above the shops of hoopers, carpenters, tailors, metal workers, tanners and shoemakers. Martin Carney was a shoemaker.

—Cobbler Carney? Mad Houlihan said when he bent down and entered the small shop.

—No, Shoemaker Carney. I never mend shoes, only make them. I leave the patchwork to the cobbler. We make a distinction in the trade.

He worked in a small bright room among bands of leather, lasts, awls, mounds of small nails and the smell of shoe dye. Against his apron he clutched a shoe, paring away the leather of a sole, with a sharp shoemaker's knife.

—I've searched Ireland for you, Mad Houlihan said.

—Well I've been here for thirty years since I left Ballinrobe. Myself and the wife Kate came east when I was finished there with a fellow called O'Donnell.

—I know.

—Well many a man came a day's distance to have a pair of boots made. But sure it takes four days from Ballinrobe and Lawless is the best shoemaker in Mayo.

—I wanted a good pair of boots, the best you can make for my foot, and he showed him the clubbed foot.

—I'll make one to fit like a glove and line it with sheepskin so that every road will feel like the floor of a king's palace.

—I'll pay you well, all the gold you ask.

—Ten gold pieces.

—That won't make you rich.

—Did you ever know a rich shoemaker? The story goes that a shoemaker refused to half-sole Saint Patrick's boots on the way to the Holy Mountain. So Saint Patrick put a curse on us, that we would work from the crack of dawn to the fall of night and be no richer for it.

Martin Carney knelt on the floor, his hands branded with black hempen thread, and measured the deformed foot, making the measurements on a leather band.

—I'm sure you have children to feed too, Mad Houlihan said.

—Eight too many. Hungry and crying and never a night's sleep until I'm driven to distraction, Shoemaker Carney said.

—And what age is the seventh child?

—A year. That's Kate, a grand girl with gold hair.

—And what of their education and upbringing?

—What education? I never went beyond the third book and as soon as the children can work they will find employment. A poor man can't have grand thoughts for his children, Shoemaker Carney told him.

So Mad Houlihan sat and had his clubbed foot measured. While Shoemaker Carney twisted it this way and that, he talked to him. He told him that he would adopt Kate, pay him a hundred gold guineas every year if he and his wife gave up claim to her, and that he would raise her to be a lady of the realm. It was beyond Shoemaker Carney's wildest dreams. Mad Houlihan left him, promising to call back for the shoes a month later. When he did, they sealed the bargain. Kate was taken away in a carriage by a nursing woman and carried west to the castle overlooking Lough Corrib.

Mad Houlihan had now his world in order. Life was as controlled as his formal French garden. Through the canal under the castle, rare shrubs and plants were still ferried. Dark ship captains carried coffers of gold and in the evenings stood above a globe of the world, accounting for their journeys across the seas. Scholars visited him bringing their knowledge and talk.

By the time Kate was sixteen she was a woman of great beauty. She spoke ten languages, played many musical instruments, discussed theology and philosophy and never had a bad thought in the world. The castle was tighter than a convent.

When she was fifteen, she began to have blood troubles. Houlihan, lost for words, called in the parish priest who sat in the room, opened a text book, looked away from her across the lake and translating a Latin text told her what was happening to her. She sat in her chair, and said nothing. When he had left, she checked his knowledge in her own Latin book. She discovered she had become a woman.

Mad Houlihan's castle was guarded by dogs and armed men. But despite his vigilance, he forgot to check the books which were carried to the castle. Kate knew more about men than a woman three times her age. From the age of fifteen she desired a man, but her control was so great that Houlihan never suspected that her mind was full of dark streets.

No one could ever tell who wrote the first ballad in praise of Kate. But by the time she was twenty her beauty had become a legend. Poets had seen her, they said, coming through the mists of the forests as they lay stupid with drink. They compared her to Venus and Helen of Troy. In the eveningtime, passing the castle, they would look up towards the tower and perhaps catch a glimpse of her, standing like a queen on the far Spanish balcony as she looked over the lake. Sometimes they heard her voice, sweet as honey or the dew of the morning, singing the sad songs of her race. There was not a hackneyed adjective or image they hadn't called out of their heads to praise her.

Again Mad Houlihan was at his annals and family trees. None but the best should kindle Kate when the time came for covering her. It took a year to chase down the best blood in Europe. The confluence of the purple bloods from the Hapsburgs, the royalty of France, the Caesars flowed through the veins of one Robert Orthega Bollingbrook, a respected Dublin rake. The last of his generation, he lived between his summer house in Dublin and his winter house in London, when he was not travelling the brothel towns of the continent. He was his own caricature. At fifty he carried a barrel of flesh under his shirt and trousers. He wallowed in deep chairs puffing for breath and, after fifty, he had to be rolled on to all beds he ever slept in. Being rich and spoiled, he never had a thought in his life. Custom made his progress through life definite.

His wealth was running out. The heaps of gold had been blown away by indulgence, wine and women. Houlihan knew all this. But it was outweighed by the single fact that he was the best sire in Ireland. So he checked his wealth and knew that in time Bollingbrook would be accessible to his wishes.

CHAPTER SIX

The fog of sleep thinned in Kelly's mind. He heard music like the flight of white pigeons in a blue sky. His eyelids opened over a fertile and infertile eye. The maggot jelly had dissolved leaving only a burnt crater, charred and dry. In remembering, Kelly could recall the face of his mother and father, but he had no fear of them, nor of the police or magistrates. His father would not take the ash plant to him anymore, or keep him from going to the crossroad dances. No longer would he listen to his mother preach at him about the evils of drink or the low blood of the women from behind the hill. He could not recall his relations scattered across half Mayo, living on poor scab land that would not grow a respectable thistle, or living between the lonely folds of esker humps, nor did he want to recall them. It was like living in Dublin all his life, and knowing nothing of the grey wet mists which rolled in across the whale humps of mean hills, lodging like fungus on lakes. It was wet, year in, year out. Men looked out small pokey windows, over half-doors for the copper shield of summer and young women in light frocks.

Looking, they had been for a thousand years.

Look they would. But it kept them dreaming and talking over wet smouldering turf. Their imaginations were soft and fertile and the seed of a market incident grew into an epic.

His eye caught the sight of his feet. They wore purple shoes sprinkled with diamonds, and he would compare nothing to them but the stars in the sky on a frosty night. He exercised his toes. They lay in a mouth of soft satin. Clearly this was not the place he had fallen asleep in, spooning porridge into his gob. Carefully, he woke up.

The room was as big as three Foresters' halls. Noble gold doors stood at the end, open. The walls were hung with tapestry, so real that Kelly might have been looking out through huge glass windows at activities in the countryside. Gods, half as big as round towers with dogs one and a half times the size of stacks of turf, were bounding across the hills, chasing deer. So real were they that if the gods talked down at him he would not be surprised. Gold and bronze shields, ornamented in scrolls and lozenges, thick as studs on hobnailed boots, hung from the beams. Around the walls on large chairs gods slept. They too were waking up slowly, their eyes cowlike and contented. Beside him sat an old man of huge stature and double girth in a soft tunic edged with red. His hair tumbled in masses over his shoulders and down his back. The lines on his face were fine and civilized, like the cream off milk, or silverware on a table.

—O'Ceallaigh, the booming voice said beside him.

—Yes, I'm still here, Kelly told him, answering to his name in Irish.

—Sleep clears the mind and leaves it even tempered, the aristocratic figure said.

—Yes, but dreams aren't powerful enough to change the bed or house or the table about which we were gathered.

—It depends on the dream and the dreamer, O'Ceallaigh, he said and he left it at that.

Talk was nibbling at the silence.

—I suppose I don't call you Tarbh anymore.

—No. Now I'm called The King.

—It's odd and I suppose when you consider it another way it's not odd, like Shauny O'Shea who said that the old castles were never built but were always there.

—A tolerable answer, the old man replied with dignity.

—It's strange nevertheless, Kelly remarked, looking for an explanation.

—Now that you ask, I might as well answer. You have white day and black nights, right and wrong, good and bad, horses and asses.

—In me walking around the roads I've seen it so and it's usual, Kelly answered.

—It is, but opposites are always crossed. Nothing is singular except essences.

—True.

—You've seen jennets?

—I have.

—Well the world in general is a jennet. It's a cross between one thing and another, the old man said.

—I'll grant you that, Kelly told him.

—Except the Celt. He's the one thing that's not tempered. And since the first Celt dragged his boat up the beaches of this country it's been like that. One day he's black with despair, the next he's bright like fire. Now he's as dark as night, then he's bright as day. There is never a twilight or a jennet for him. That's why he'll fail. No plant ever survived unless it was crossed and purebreds are mad because they have no centre, the old man said.

It was a long talk of explanation and Kelly took it all in and chewed on it like good grass.

Large holes were eaten in the silence now.

—Give me a look at that eye of yours, the King said, taking Kelly's jaw in his hand and twisting his face over to him.

—That's a bad eye you got there, like a shough with rotten potatoes.

—I'm off balance for life, like a slanted cursing stone, Kelly complained.

—Well now, maybe there is a cure for it, but only a witch in Lapland could give you a new eye, which she would have to thumb out of a seal.

—I'd be maimed for life looking out on fields with the eye of a man and the eye of a seal; one looking at growing grass, brown clamps of turf and the other staring out looking for a glimpse of the sea. And maybe it would divide my mind like the cow with two heads that didn't know which road to take. One day I'd want to walk inland and the next I'd be running along the wild places of Achill or Belmullet where there is rough horshing between the sea and the slimy rocks, Kelly said, thinking of the division in his soul.

—No. It's not what I intended as I'm not a craftsman in the replacement of eyes. But I'll give you a good substitute.

You'll bear a blank eye back with you, for it was the price you had to pay for coming the long journey, like twopence at a toll-bridge. But this stone carries the qualities of your mind and its running colours never rest. It will be red in anger, white in love, black in despair, and spiralling like the markings on the old stones when you are angry, the King told him.

—It's unusual.

—But most things from now on will be usual, Kelly, and you will drive such fear into men's minds when you take the notion and boil in anger, they will fly away down the small roads like midges.

While he spoke he took a heavy ring from his finger, carrying an almond-shaped stone. He prised the stone from its gold bed, put it to Kelly's eye and thumbed it deep into the socket. It was soft and cool like honey dripping from the honeycomb. The memory of Mickey O'Gara's forge and the comet of pain sparks went forever. Kelly winked a few times to get used to it and then looked down the hall, filled with talk.

Kelly sat in the splendour of lights. His mind was in no turmoil as it used to be when he waited outside the confession box of the priests down from Dublin to preach the missions. Then he would sit humped over the seat looking at the worn kneeling-plank, with shiny nailheads, going through his sins. And always his mind was disturbed with the sixth commandment. There was small matter in all the sins except this one and no dodging it. He always found it hard to find words to describe the desires that flooded into his mind the time he came by Mary Corley pissing in a ditch, the day of the haymaking, or the thoughts that came into his head and the young women walking up the aisle of a church to the top seats the morning of Sunday Mass. Twice he had slipped out of the church and ran across the meadows with delight, unable to bring himself to the confession box.

The light clothes on his body were as white and soft as bog cotton, or putting his bum deep in the down of a mattress. He forgot his scrapy corduroy breeches and the rough flannel shirt he wore summer and winter.

His net was now full of fish.

—It's a grand thing to be living ever and always like this not bothering about night or day or the price of cattle, Kelly told the King.

—It's alright, Kelly, but I'm beginning to creak a bit. My blood has grown sluggish and thick, and the fine wine and the soft fruit rasp my tongue. It's nearly time for me to be leaving all this, and my spirit taking the boat across the black water, to the fields we have staked out in the land of the Dead. This is only a half-life here. It's a dream that runs across your mind and you asleep. And there is many another one in the hall that will come after me, for all the famous names in the old stories are sitting down there in front of you, the King told him.

—You have years in you yet. I knew a woman who lived to be a hundred and four and she died only because a bit of meat got stuck in her throat of a Friday, though she didn't know it was a Friday then, but discovered it when she had it half way down her gullet, Kelly said in consolation.

—No, Kelly, I'm already dead in one way of speaking. Soon they will be carrying my body across country to a mound on a hill overlooking a broad river bed. They will carry it between scotched pillars into a stone womb and there will be great wailing. But don't think too closely about decaying flesh, Kelly. It gives you a sad soul and you are a young man, the King said solemnly.

—We'll turn our thoughts from death and switch them down the hall towards all the company, Kelly directed him.

The King snapped his fingers and there was a granary of silence. The side doors opened and ten harpers entered. They sat on a platform in the middle of the hall and began to race their hands across the strings like mice skittering between stubble. Kelly had never heard anything like it in his life. They were serious harpers, not the mean faced men who play for coppers. When they were finished the King took a gold cup and slung it down the hall to the eldest harper. They left the room and a juggler came in with a leather bag. To the common eye it looked empty but when he put in his hand he took out a sword, and a duck and a dog. The dog ran around the floor balancing the sword on its nose, while the duck ran after him dropping gold eggs and squeaking. The juggler ran after the duck, catching the eggs as they dropped, and threw them up into the air juggling them into forty different patterns. When the duck had laid a hundred eggs and the juggler was tired tossing them this way and that, he threw them back to the duck and she snapped them into her mouth and down her throat without making any enlargement to her proportions.

—I've never seen the beating of that for a trick, Kelly said, and I don't believe there is the equal to it in the four corners of Ireland, no matter how far a man walked.

Then an old man made his appearance with a beard as long as a sheaf of oats, white and grey and white and grey. His eyes were drooping and wet with misery. He stared out into the uncertain distance and sang the genealogical trees, telling where every god came from and where every god fitted in. The last flower on the tree was Kelly. It all took a sleepy five hours as he droned on like a leaky bagpipes with wet reeds. When he was done, they were all asleep. He was asleep himself. Two footmen came and carried him from the hall.

While they were being entertained, servants were feeding them with all types of meat, wine and nuts. Kelly was never so replete in his life.

—Throw the doors open, it's too warm here, the King ordered.

The footsoldiers threw the doors open. Evening was smouldering in the sky. The air was warm and tanged with the sea. They could hear the pout mutter of the waves lapping and fluttering along a beach, and the sound of the seals in conversation.

There was a patter of horse hooves on the sea, then on sand, then on firm ground. A woman stood at the door. She entered and walked up the hall like a queen. She was tall, her hair blond and sea-blown about her. Her fine skin was pear soft, her gown sea green. Kelly noticed how strong and full her body was with a surplus of golden flesh for kneading fingers. She had the disdain of the thoroughbred at the door of a dirty stable. She sat beside the King, took a gold bowl of wine and sipped at it. After the wonder of her appearance there was talk again.

Kelly was now a finished god. Fine delight was as natural to him as a cow coming through a gate to be milked. They could send the loudest roarers from Dublin to preach the mission and they would make no impression on him.

——There are plenty of coals in that grate, Kelly said to the King, pointing to the woman.

——That one has such a thirst for men that a field of them lined up with their trousers off would not take the edge off her, the King told him.

Kelly could not take his eyes off her. Her breasts were as big as turnips and as soft, he thought, as the heart of young cabbage. And he would swear that the tops of her tits were as big as thumbs and them excited. He liked fine women and not young half-starved stringers that would disappear if they turned sideways.

——Who's your man there with the gammy eye? she asked.

——That's the bold Kelly, the King said.

——We're not related to any Kellys, she said.

——This Kelly is one of our own, the last and freshest of them.

——I like fresh men, she said directly.

——And I'd say nothing myself to pinching your bum, Kelly said, overhearing the talk and speaking out what was in his mind.

——You talk I see, she said.

——And back any talk by action, if the notion took me, he told her.

——Where did you come from?

——From Mickey O'Gara's forge five thousand years ago.

——Where?

——North Mayo.

——A bleak place.

——We never choose where we are dropped, Kelly told her.

——You're a fair one with the tongue.

——A fellow has to be to protect himself, he told her.

Kelly held his own. Talk came easy to him and he never let a woman away with the last word. But he could hazard a guess that she was taking to him and had no objections to his stoking her fire and maybe kindling a flame.

——Tell me this now and tell me no lie, Kelly asked, but

do you recall all that blackness and squalor a few hours back? It doesn't add up or balance out, Kelly told the King.

—That, Kelly, was the blackness of your nature and you can never forget it. You might kennel it for a time but the meat hunger and the marrow pain will unleash the hungry dogs in your belly, the King told him.

—And I'll carry it all this with me? Kelly asked.

—Yes, you'll carry it all about with you. It's as fixed as the mountains in the land.

—So it will come again and again, the black and white, swinging one way and then another, Kelly stated.

—It will, the King said.

—It's a curse, he remarked.

—Yes, it's a curse, but all life is uneven. The gods have no smooth answer. Nothing will lock the black to white or temper iron with gold.

—Give over that long talk. Of course you lock things together. And if you're ready you might have the key that would lock my door for the wind is whistling down the passage, the woman said.

She rose and left the room. Kelly followed. Behind them the sound of talk was stifled by the yawning door. She had a pavilion of wind-running silk pegged on the shore. A black woman opened the flap and they walked inside, passed through an outer passage into a circular room with a luxurious bed, hung with a canopy.

The black woman stood beside her and took the silk from her body stitch by stitch, veil by veil, until she stood naked in front of him, flesh like soft pears, hair, blond tufted, her boobs as big as turnips, as he had visualised. She yawned sensually and lay on the bed.

—Well, Kelly, everything your eye roves over is fair? she asked.

—Be Cripes it is, mam, he said, his opal eye pulsing from red to white.

—Well what in the hell are you waiting for, like an ass looking over a stone wall? I'm not a stone Venus that never moved a limb. Will you take off your trousers.

—Oh begod I will, mam, and with dancing drunk fingers he pulled down his trousers. But his legs got muddled up and he tripped banging his nose off the ground. A jet of blood shot onto his lip.

He staggered up and untwisted his Celtic trousers and stepped out of it. He pulled off his silk shirt roaring *Alleliu* and took a buckleap bedwards, like a duck shot in flight.

Time is relative. Kelly was airborne and primed. The time of his flight could have been as long as it took the first sea creature to organise itself and crawl shorewards. Or he could have been preserved in amber for a million years.

The silk of the world shredded, and turned to penetential sacking. The warm wind so soft on his body became a northern gale which nearly skinned his airborne bum. The sea so feminine and fluttery went into a rage, crashing and tearing and bellowing like a penned bull. The light was snuffed out. He landed on a bed of rough heather, pricky and tearing.

—I've done an injury to meself, he roared, I've scraped the cover off me balls.

Before he could count genital or general injury the hag was on top of him straddling him. She was a flat chested, bony-kneed crone, her skeletal hands and limbs flailing the chaff from his wheat. She had him pinned to the hard ground. She stenched her passion at him through black teeth.

—The bloody thing was too good, Kelly thought lucidly for a moment. Her dry lips were barnacled to his, pumping plague to the back of his gullet, her spare knockety behind pumping up and down searching for oil.

—Leave off, leave off or you'll have me worn out.

She kept drilling. The door of the hut burst open and twelve or thirteen hags ran in screaming and screeching, carrying lights. They danced about on starved legs, croaking like corncrakes and whineying like mares. Kelly's eyes began to blaze red. He grabbed a stone from the floor and mashed her face, feeding gum and teeth into her mouth.

She staggered off her straddle and Kelly's pin came loose. He was up and them about him. He kicked them where he ought not, but it was their love and his war. He ran through the door and them after him. Across bog and moor he ran. They caught him when he tripped in a bog hole. They were on top of him, a pyramid of deprived females.

Kelly thought he was done for. If they captured him they would surely put him to stud and there was no knowing but he might die a young man from rupture. He bundled up the energy inside him for one final onslaught. He would burst his bladder in an attempt to shift the mass of writhing cackle.

There was turmoil at the base of his skull sucking him apart. A giant vortex dragged him this way and that up through a dark lake.

He broke surface like a twisted fart.

CHAPTER SEVEN

The frieze of faces above Kelly looked down at the chained figure wondering if they had killed or cured.

—I'd swear by Jupiter, Cray stated, that we have perpetrated a murder.

O'Shaughnessy stethoscoped his ear to Kelly's chest and winked an eye in concentration.

—His heart has stopped and if it's pounding, it's pounding real slow like a train coming into a station.

—We'll surely end up in Castlebar Jail for murder for this, a legalist droned.

—Whist. He's easy got rid of in a bog hole. There are enough bog holes in these parts to swallow a regiment and no one would find them in a thousand years, Crane told them.

They looked at O'Gara, unnoticed since he stood above Kelly, the strongest man in the locality ready to lunge a poker in his eye. He was growing grey, giving out slow sighs which suggested that he too was dying.

—Bring over the torch until we see O'Gara, somebody commanded.

Light flickered across O'Gara's grandfather, he looked so old, his hair albino white, skin shrivelled, fingers twitching without co-ordination.

—'Tis strange. 'Tis passing strange, the sight of him there and all his days rushed into one night, Fowler Murtagh said.

—Are you alright, O'Gara? somebody asked.

—Take me indoors to bed. Lay me between sheets. The strength is drained out of me. I saw things tonight that no man should talk about.

They grabbed him by arms and legs and shuffled him across the dark yard to his wife Mary Ellen.

—That's not the man I married. It's his father, she told the men.

She was a young woman, jealous that his strength had been drained from him by a poker.

—Remember, Mary Ellen, the 'for better and for worse bit'. Well this is the worse bit, Dick Ryan said.

—I'll remember nothing. Cart him down to the graveyard where he belongs for I'll not lie with a withered auld man. I want no invalid in my bed.

—Care for him while you can, Mary Ellen. Signs are that he won't be in the land of the living for long, they told her.

—'Twas from tampering with natural matters that you brought the disaster about, she said when she heard the story.

—We had to do it, Mary Ellen. There were no two ways about it. The maggot would have been the death of every parish in Ireland, Crane told her.

—It's the priest you should have called with all the powers in his Latin book, Mary Ellen told them.

—There are certain things, Mary Ellen, that the Pope himself couldn't rectify, even if all he says is true, Dick Ryan said.

They heard horse snorts from the forge. Hurrying back, they found Kelly resuscitating, his chest big as a barrel, his breathing heavy and regular. He drew in air and blew it out. His hair had reddened and thickened. The brand had fallen from his eye leaving a burnt hole. Inarticulate raimeis was coming from his throat as he sweated agony.

—'Tis the devil's doing, whatever in the world is happening. That isn't Kelly at all, Cray stated.

Kelly groaned heavily, twisting his head this way and that. They were all clearly startled, though not surprised at the transformation of Kelly. They were the victims of their own overpractised imaginations, mixing myth with reality, no partition dividing either world.

—If he lives to tell about it, it is one of the wonders of the natural world like the calf with two heads or the sow that dropped the foal in me father's time, O'Shaughnessy said.

Somebody was talking about it being the sixth proof of

the existence of God.

They stared, stricken. Kelly was acting up, heaving harder, hampered by rusty chains.

——It could be a foreign disease of which they die in the centre of Africa, Crane said.

——What do you know about such diseases? Dick Ryan asked.

——I read a book once and it was in it, O'Shaughnessy said.

——Well he reminds me of the story of Cuchulainn bound to the rock and the crow or some such bird on his shoulder, Crane said.

——Like the raven in the poem I was telling you about, a bystander added.

——Some suchlike.

——We might as well sit and wait, a patient voice suggested.

——Throw a bit of slack in the fire and blow it to life.

Riordan, with the red nose, did. It showered up a galaxy of sparks, which lit every corner of the forge for a moment. Then there was a private glow of light again. They sat in a ring, anvil as sacrificial altar, fire purging the darkness, shadows licking across the wet sweaty chest of Kelly. In the half-light the gathering looked like doctors at a slow, speculative autopsy, studying the corpse from a variety of angles.

——Sing an amhrán, Seamus, somebody told Hamrock.

——In the old fashion? he asked.

——Yes and fair dos to you, lad, Riordan encouraged.

Seamus ploughed his throat and harrowed it with spittle.

——I'm out of practice, he complained, I'd need a drop of the craytur to oil me vocal cords and put me in proper fettle.

——No need, Seamus, when you take it in your head to sing, Cray said.

After the traditional bit of encouragement to sing, he started. He droned on in his best Armenian voice. It was a fine skirl of music, full of melancholy. A young lady had been got in the family way by a buck of the manor, who was unfaithful and married another. She threw herself from a cliff and died, her fine body mashed against the black rocks. It satisfied a morbid instinct in them that they carried their

decrepid souls about in patched, dry soulbags, while someone bearing their memories of youth and summertime carried
green life to death on the rocks.

The song stopped and their imaginations carried on. There
was a space of silence for a minute as they gathered the
mangled body of the lady and buried her on a low, sandy
graveyard about a ruined monastery.

After the bagpipes' skirl of music from Hamrock they
began to tell stories of weddings and wakes, of fellows who
went to England, America, and Alaska. Their pace was wake
pace, thoughtful and slow. Sometimes it did not move at all,
haltered as it is out in the fields of eternity. The landscape,
whin-yellow, called the pace. If time fell into a canter, they
all might fall off the world.

—What day of the week is it be way of interruption?
asked Cray.

They thought for a while.

—It might be a Thursday seeing that the fair was on
Tuesday.

—No, the fair was on Wednesday and it's Friday now and
any man who eats meat today will have to go to the feet of
the bishop himself, O'Shaughnessy said.

—That would knock you back a pound or two, Riordan
told them.

—It's an expensive type of transgression, O'Shaughnessy
said.

They stood and sat about the chained figure of Kelly
like the surgeons in the picture by Rembrandt about the
chalky corpse. By now Kelly was coming back from the dark
pilgrimage in the cisterns of his mind. He grunted and heaved
at his chains, burning them into his expanded chest. They
snapped apart and Kelly was free.

He was conscious of the stinging, cauterized eye. His
throat was wooden and dry, fibrous like a bamboo pole. He
shook himself, gripped the anvil and threw it from him. He
rushed from the forge and into the darkness. A cuticle of
moon and bright stars gave some phosphorescence to the
night.

Roaring, Kelly ran through the small village, his thirst and
hunger driving him on, pushing towards drink and meat.

There was foamy froth on his lips. Every inch of his body was like dry lime. His stomach was hungry after its journey.

He saw barrels of porter stacked outside Healy's pub, sitting in delayed judgement. He scooped one under his arm and continued running.

Ownie Brown's pigs had stopped grunting for the night and lay snouting contentment in dirty styes. Kelly scented the pig shit on the wind and followed the trail. He battered down the door, foraged among the squealing pigs until he found a soft sow, tucked her under his arm and rushed down the street again. He looked up at the silhouette of Croman Hill, boggy-sided and secret. He made for the hill.

Windows and doors of the village were thrown open, angry sleepers wondering at the mixture of roaring from Kelly and the ignorant grunts of the sow. They saw a tail of bony old men running down from O'Gara's forge, following the noise at the confused distance.

—What in God's name has you on the street at this hour of night, Father Rance asked, when every decent man is at home between sheets? What are you doing disturbing the night's sleep of the town?

Peeler O'Rourke, his dignity hung on a nail at the back of the door, woke from a peaceful sleep. He tugged on his stiff blue trousers, his sweat-hardened, worsted socks, muttered grumpy protests to the hump of his wife wallwards. Her imagination was chewing dry grass in some dreamy field or other.

—What in the blazes hell do they have to come between a man and his sleep? The limping idiots should be miles out of town by now, he said.

His peak-cap pointing eastwards towards the unrisen sun, he buckled on his belt under the years of an easy paunch, scratched the pimples on his back and heaved himself door-wards.

—What's the roaring about? What's the roaring about? Has there been a murder or something? he called, bolting down the street. The night stung precision into his eyes. He saw the shivering mass of men at the door of the presbytery, like a crowd of reprobates gabbling a communal confession.

—What in the name of all that's high and holy has ye out

on the streets? I should land you all down in the cell. Has some decent woman been assaulted?

——'Tis worse than that. 'Tis worse than that, Kelly has gone stark raving mad. If he's not put in the lunatic asylum, he'll do someone a grievous harm. There is no knowing under heaven what fearful damage will be done to stone walls and turf stacks and him going the way he went, Crane told Peeler O'Rourke.

——But Kelly is only a maggot-eaten stem of a man, Peeler O'Rourke said.

——He was. He was. Up to tonight. Till O'Gara dragged him in felons' chains down to the forge and tried to hammer a job on that eye of his. We thought he was killed until he started to recover rapid. He ran from the forge cursing Pope, Priest and the Queen of England, Riordan said.

——You're all drunk, Father Rance told them.

——Oh Cripes no, Father, Cray said, the devil himself got into the man. Such changes took place that would have to be seen to be believed. I wouldn't credit it unless I saw it with my own two eyes. Without a word of a lie he grew to be twice the man he was and his hair went savage red like rust on a galvanized shed. And his tools, if you'll excuse the expression, Father, became far outsized like those of Doran's bull.

——You could go to every agricultural show in the country and not see the likes of them under any animal, O'Shaughnessy said.

——'Tis true, 'tis very true, 'tis very very true, they Greek-chorused at Peeler O'Rourke.

——And the last we saw of him was tearing up to Croman Hill bog, a barrel of porter under one elbow and a squealing pig under the other, and him raving and roaring. We saw things tonight that would strike fear into any wholesome normal man, they said.

——We'll wait for the dawn, Peeler O'Rourke said, and we'll check your story against the daylight.

——I think it is the only sensible measure to take, Father Rance chimed in.

It sounded good advice, seeing that it came from two intelligent men. So they turned their heads homewards and huddled together for protection.

—Did it happen or did me eyes deceive me? Hamrock asked.

—It happened alright. But I have me fears that this is only the beginning. I could swear that I saw the ugly face of the devil himself looking down through the hole of the forge roof grinning at me with white teeth, Cray told them.

—If the lad below has a hand in it, you can be on the look out, O'Shaughnessy said.

—There is no bull in Ireland that carries the likes of Kelly's about with him, Crane remarked.

—But he has the shoulders to carry them, Riordan added.

—'Tis a new trousers with raincoat buttons he'll be needing, Crane told them.

—He will indeed. Some men have such gifts, said a decayed figure at the edge of the crowd, 'tis fair damage he'll do to the women of Ireland. No one will be safe from him.

—One should never tamper with the forces of nature, or throw them out of proportion. It is likely to throw the elements into confusion, Hamrock said solemnly.

No sooner said than done. A heavy whale of cloud, pregnant with rain, sailed between the cuticle moon and the village. A harpoon of jagged lightning flittered the darkness and plunged into the crowd. Rumbling thunder with ponderous wheels rutted across the sky. The belly of cloud discharged a deluge of rain, cascading down on roofs and streets with metal hooves. It was a wild carnival of stinging rain, shot through with shaft after shaft of lightning, which danced on the street.

The figures ran different ways from the barbed lightning, calling for divine protection.

The lightning cleared the town of people, the thunder silenced nagging wives, the deluge of rain cleared the Y-shaped market place of dung, and of the day's memories. Now the night sky was clear, stars shining again, the moon giving slight, unobtrusive light.

So the day and half the night, full of events, finished in the town. Old men carried their memories, muttering home to bed. Women flopped in beside snoring husbands, the pigs in Ownie Brown's sty settled in the gutter snoring sideways, hens put their heads under their wings and peace fluttered over the roofs.

Kelly was above it all. He tethered the sow by its tail to a whin bush. He placed the barrel of porter on a rock beside a hut, floored with crushed heather. He tore off his clothes and rushed down to the dark waters under Croman Hill. With strong strokes he went down through the sinister, dead depths. His dry body drank in the water, the cold bit into the socket of his eye. Steam lifted from the lake. The pain deadened. It was cool now and when he felt the gap of his eye it was filled with a hard opal stone. Free from pain, he broke the surface and cavorted like a happy dolphin.

Later he stood naked on the top of the hill, looking over the sleepy world lit by a weak dawn. He was conscious of his power to conquer, confuse, delight and sadden.

Having looked at the world beneath him, he prepared his meal. He gutted and spitted the pig, setting it to roast over a fire. And while he was waiting for it to roast under oak roots, he knocked open the barrel and held it to his mouth. It was black and strong like tar, furring his stomach with content. There he tore the oak-toned meat asunder and ate it, feeding his wide appetite. He picked the crubeens and ribs with discrimination and doused the mouthfuls of meat with porter.

Tomorrow was climbing over the fence of the horizon. Well he would take tomorrows as they came, easy that the world was a small place and the minds of people smaller still. He could rove now at will like an ass grazing the long acre at the side of the road. He could go this way and that way and the devil in hell could not stop him.

When he finished the sow, he threw the bones into the fire, kicked the wooden barrel apart and threw it also on top of the burning bones. Then he went into the hut, wrapped himself and fell asleep.

CHAPTER EIGHT

Faustus MacGinty was three feet high. He grew to that stature and stopped, so to him the world was twice as big as it was. When he went to Scaragh school, the master said he had one of the brightest wits in Ireland for a lad of his age or a man of his size.

——You have the biggest head I've ever seen, lad, the teacher said to him when he called him to inscribe his name on the roll.

——It wasn't of my doing, sir. I wasn't sitting at a wall looking at me making in some ditch or other, Faustus answered back in a thin voice.

——That's rough language for a young fellow. Where did you pick up terms like that? the teacher inquired.

——Here and there and me ears cocked like John Thomas, he told him.

——You'll have to change here, lad. You can't be that free with your tongue. What's your name?

——Faustus MacGinty.

——Faustus MacGinty?

——Yes, Faustus MacGinty.

——Hard to find Irish for that, and the master scratched his head. I know, we'll call you Seadhna MacGinty after the man in the story who sold his soul to the devil. Wasn't that fast thinking on my part? the teacher said with a narrow smirk on his face.

——Fast enough.

——What age are you?

——Five, sir. Maybe six. I'm neither sure of the year nor the day.

——How's that?

——I was picked up on the side of a ditch by a travelling tinsmith and his wife and they left me in the care of Widow Magher.

——I'll invent a date and hold to it, and the master delivered him on the eighth of January.

——Remember. You were born on the eighth of January.

The class were whispering behind their books.

——Silence, you fools, or I'll raise welts on you. Work hard at the books and you might get a job in one of the big towns or maybe in Dublin, he advised.

The class settled into the books again.

——You know what you come to school for? the teacher asked.

——To learn, sir.

——Yes to learn, so you can get a good job. You're on the first rung of the ladder now and if you hold steady you can climb to the top and get a post that is permanent and pensionable.

He delivered this sermon over the heads of every new arrival. Faustus held the equilibrium of his face and was not impressed.

——See that stick, the master said, holding a knotty cudgel above his head. If anyone steps out of line I'll raise welts on his backside.

He beat the air, raising welts on it.

——Tell me now, do you know anything at all, for we'll have to find out what book to put you in.

——A bit.

——Can you recite poetry?

——A bit. Shakespeare?

——What bit of Shakespeare?

——It depends on what your taste is, comedy, tragedy, history.

——Do you know the bit beginning To be or not to be, that is the question?

——Act III, Scene 1.

——Go ahead.

He went ahead. The master listened in surprise knowing

that he was up against something he had not encountered before.

——Where did you learn that?

——In a book I bought from a chapman passing the road.

——Do you know anything besides English?

——I do, sir, lumps of Latin.

——What type of Latin?

——Classical Latin.

——Recite some.

He did.

——I don't say I can follow you, but it sounds lovely. The parish priest is a fair hand at the Latin and the Greek. He'd know.

——I recite in Greek too, Faustus said.

——That's beyond me, the teacher said.

——It's easy enough when you get in on the alphabet and verbs.

——I suppose you don't know any other languages.

——Enough Swahili to get me by if I found myself in Africa.

——How about sums?

——I can cypher. I can do the five books of Euclid with the cuts, algebra, measure fields and name out the stars.

——You better sit at the back and take out some book of your own liking for you're way ahead of the rest and I'll get the parish priest to have a talk with you.

Schoolmaster MacGrath put Faustus in the back seat by himself. He was hidden from the rest of the class by a ditch of eighteen year old idiots who were comprehending writing and reading. Faustus took out a copy of Virgil and decided to run through the first five books before dinner. He was contented in the passageway between the windows and the row of wide backs and patched trousers.

A week later the parish priest was passing by the school and called. There was a reverent shuffle of boots and squeak of bench hinges when he opened the door.

——God be with you, he said in Irish.

——God and Patrick and Brigid, and Colmcille with you too Father, they monotoned.

Faustus MacGinty was aware of the priest. He sat, his

hands holding his big head above a book.

—Where's the prodigy? he asked in banter.

—Down here, father, down here, father, the last row chimed.

The priest scanned the wall of ignorant faces at the end of the room. Between them they might make up one brain.

—Down here, Father, behind us, they clarified.

The priest went down and discovered the corridor between their backs and the window. Faustus never noticed him.

—MacGinty, will you salute the priest, schoolmaster MacGrath said.

Faustus looked up. He looked back at the book again, licked a finger, turned over a page.

—Young man, said Schoolmaster MacGrath, stand up in the presence of his reverence.

—And why should I? he asked.

—And why shouldn't you?

—Well I've studied all the rubrics and rituals and I'll bet you can't give me page and paragraph where it states specifically in Church Latin that I should stand up when a priest enters a national school, he said in a legal voice.

—I told you, Father, he's a genius. He even knows a bit of African, schoolmaster MacGrath said.

—They say you know Latin, the priest stated.

—I do.

—Recite a bit.

He recited an ode by Ovid.

—Would the genius translate for the benefit of the class that we might all be a little wiser as a result, schoolmaster MacGrath said.

—No. That's alright now. You wouldn't be any wiser as a result, the priest said solemnly.

—You shouldn't be saying dirty things like that out loud in Latin, son. You should spend your time better, learning your catechism, the priest told him.

—What catechism?

—The catechism with the green paper cover.

—But that's not a catechism, that's only the summary of a catechism. What I'm looking for now is the Summa Theologica but schoolmaster MacGrath never heard of it,

Faustus said.

——I heard of it alright, Father, but I can't lay my hands on it at home. I must have lent it to somebody or other.

——Well, son, if it's the Summa Theologica you want, I'll bring two of these hod carriers here up to the presbytery and they can carry the set down. Read it and tell me what you think about it, he told him.

The priest left, stirred by wonder, for there was no knowing but Faustus MacGinty was either another Aquinas or a budding schismatic who would divide the faithful and lead acres of them astray.

——MacGinty, Paddy Paudge Joyce whispered, will you translate that Latin poetry out in the lavatory afterwards?

He did.

——God Almighty, I never heard anything like it in me life and you mean to say that you're reading that sort of stuff at the back of the class and the rest of us doing sums and grammar?

——Yes.

——Is there any chance you would teach me Latin on the quiet and mark the passages in pieces of books which might interest me?

——For you, Joyce, learning Latin would be like ploughing the Rocks of Bawn. It would take you eight hundred years to master it.

Joyce's face fell to the lavatory.

——'Tis sad, he said.

——Sure I know, Faustus said, the world is full of the fears of things.

When they returned after the break there was a barrow-load of books in Faustus MacGinty's corridor.

——Don't tell me that one man wrote these? Master MacGrath asked.

——He did indeed, six hundred years ago, Faustus told him.

The master took up one and let it fall apart.

——Latin?

——Church Latin.

——How did you know about them?

——I keep my ears cocked, Faustus said, like a duck's

bum.

—If that duck keeps his bum cocked as long as you keep your ears, he must have a right cold in it.

—A duck's bum is waterproof, Faustus told him.

—Well you learn a bit every day. If it's not about the Latin poems, it's about the wonders of the natural world.

—It's true, sir.

—Where's Pernambuco? the schoolmaster asked.

—I don't know, Faustus replied.

—There you are, you might know something but you don't know everything. You study them books and I'll run over the tables with these fellows, and he went up the classroom pleased that Faustus MacGinty didn't know where Pernambuco was.

—Well some know one thing and others know another thing, Master MacGrath said to himself.

Joyce passed around his translation of Ovid at dinnertime between sandwich gulps. He added a bit and by the time he was finished the crowd about him could see some purpose to education. Every day in the lavatory Faustus would have to recite a bit of Latin poetry and translate it. Later they dispensed with the sonorities of Latin and made him get directly to the translation. When they left school a year later they were all versed in Roman culture and could quote good translations by heart.

He spent thirteen years at school. His corridor was marked out for him and he lived in privacy. Periodically the schoolmater would come down and ask him where an obscure village in India or South America was, but outside that he browsed in peace through every parish priest's library in Munster. His voice never broke at fourteen, but no one noticed on account of his size. Towards the end of his thirteenth year the parish priest came into the classroom and sat down beside him.

—You've read a fair bit since you came in the classroom door thirteen years ago.

—There are fields of books I didn't even touch yet, Faustus told the priest.

—I know where there are fields of books, the priest said.

—You do?

——Yes, in a place called Maynooth.

——That's where the finest brains in Ireland go? Faustus asked.

——That's right. On your way out of Dublin on your way to Mullingar you will see them any day inside the wall reading out of books, dressed in black and not a worry on them.

——Acres of books you tell me.

——It's so, but you go there with a general purpose in mind.

——I know what you're getting at, Father.

——You do?

——Yes.

——Now tell me have you any great interest in girls?

——Well not that great. They are nice enough to look at done out of a Sunday.

——Well Sunday or Monday you won't see them in Maynooth.

——I know, but the hunger I suffer from is inside my head.

——I think you should give Maynooth a try.

——I will.

He did.

He walked through the gate at the end of a summer, in a black suit, dragging a heavy case across the cobbles. He was a wonder to the brawny, ascetic seminarians. They latched their eyes on to him, thinking he was an altar server astray in the cloister. He said very little. But everyday he made his way to the library, took down a handful of books and started reading. There was no end to knowledge he thought. There were books on everything and he doubted if he could ever get to the bottom of it all.

He said nothing for a year. He listened. He doubted. He read. It was at this time that his mind began to fall asunder. He could not keep pace with all the knowledge in the library. So he learned to read with each individual eye, devouring the contents of two books at once. Then he starved himself of sleep and late and early was hooped over the reading desk in the library. A cold, mad glitter came into his eye. He began to doubt more. A dormant stutter grew in his mouth. Ideas ran like barking dogs across his mind and he could not tether them with the words. So it took him half an hour to stammer out a question and by the time he had made himself clear it was time for dinner and a thousand other ideas were bubbling in his head.

It was discovered that he had only one dangler. He never felt the nail in the flesh like others. His heart had no reason. Like Origen he was lobsided, too full of thought, and could never stoop to the sensual troubles of the world.

So the faculty congregated in a large oak room, with solemn churchmen in fifth-rate portraits looking down on them. They decided that the Levite MacGinty would never make a presbyter for the following reasons. Medically he was ballsed up. You cannot have a mens sana without a corpora sana. With a dangler absent, he was only half a man. He was biased against reality. Any man so constituted could not sensate properly, which affects concepts, which affects judgment. The aspirant had no humour. And God knows, that the universe is such a tangle that any man who never thought was confronted with black despair and if he cannot laugh he will crack. No one had ever heard a cackle of laughter from Faustus. The fifth-rate portraits sighed with relief when the three points were inscribed in Latin.

Faustus wasn't disturbed unduly when he was told to leave. He believed somewhere in the rooms of his mind that one place was equal to another. However he had to live.

An eccentric count who heard of Faustus MacGinty's plight employed him to go around Ireland and collect Latin tombstone inscriptions. He wished to write a book for private circulation on this matter and needed a good Latinist to do research for him when he was cemented to an armchair by gout. So Faustus started on his journey around Ireland, carrying a good ordnance map in his pocket. He went through the small towns and villages. He brought very little with him, his pipe and tobacco, a few books, a scraper for scraping moss from recumbent gravestones, a notebook and a pencil. It was work that would take up half a lifetime, but it gave him the freedom of his feet and took him away from books. He dropped out of sight for five or six years until he turned up later in Belmullet.

CHAPTER NINE

Leibide Ludden was quarried dull. He was also of doubtful origin. The dame herself came from a run of low wits and she could not account for extra weight seven months gone.
—Wind from wet potatoes, she complained, gassing up in my stomach.
—Faith that's not a wind complaint you have got there and you'll have to take more than bicarbonate soda to get rid of it. It's not a thing that you can fart easily away, a neighbour said.
It was a commonality of talk about the countryside that Big Nell Ludden at thirty-six was carrying a weight of trouble under her dugs. The priest heard about it. So one day when the sky looked settled, he set out up the mountainside to the cottage. He sized up the situation when he saw her and sent for the doctor. Eyes behind windows and from the darkness of half-doors watched.
—It was no harm that the priest caught up with Big Nell because there wasn't a travelling man in the country who didn't make his way to the house under the cover of night, they said.
—Nell, said the doctor, I have big news for you.
—You have, have you?
—Yes. You're expecting.
—A what?
—Do you see the sow out there in the yard?
—Yes.
—Do you understand now?
—No.

——One of these days something will stir and you'll have a child on your lap.

——Oh I see, she said, so it's more than potato wind?

——It's more than potato wind, Nell.

After the revelation Old Dan Ludden and the doctor set about discovering the father.

——Think hard, girl, for we must trace him down, they said.

——Sure I can't think, father, except it was Tinker Maher or Fiddler MacGarry or the knacker man that came to take away the dead ass.

——Is that all?

——There were others off and on.

——Did they assault you?

——Well it depends what you mean by assault. They pulled down their trousers for the job. They never bothered hanging them on the end of the bed like a banking man might, but into bed as fast as skitter from your arse.

——Did you encourage them?

——Well, no. A bit of talk and carry on. One thing led to another.

There was a twinkle of reverie in her squint eye.

——Tell me honestly, daughter, how long has this been going on?

——'Tis not that I could say for certain between one thing and another. Twenty years, give or take a year.

——It's a grevious sin, a grevious sin, the priest told her.

——'Tisn't for the cow or pig, and a great sense of enlightenment on their faces and them at it.

——Now, Nell, there is a difference, the priest began.

——There is more likeness than difference, she said.

——It's a theological difference, if you see what I mean.

——Well to tell the truth, I don't, she replied.

——Have reverence for the holy priest of God, daughter, Old Dan Ludden roared, brandishing a spiked blackthorn over her head.

——I can't see what part he plays in me transactions. As I say it was no great happening. It may not have been between clean sheets or in a honeymoon hotel in Galway or Achill, but we went about it the same way.

Intellectual and moral fury flared in the priest's mind. He ramshackled it for simple, hard words, but only long, wordy definitions came to him. He was up against something outside the rule of Rome, and which went back far further if only he could disentangle it.

—It's a shame, he told her.

—It might be, but I knocked a fair auld kick out of it, she said.

Neither priest nor doctor could chip the marble of her ignorance. So they left her and walked down the hungry hill, and moved along the road to the town where a church spire indicated Christian roots.

Nell went back to kneading bread, talking now and then to the load within her.

The grandfather, Dan Ludden, felt easy when the priest and doctor had left. He had to side with them because he feared the power of the priest over his soul and the doctor over his body. But in the end what did they know, down there in the far town between silk sheets and meat on the table every day. They didn't live in the brooding closeness of the hills where you take your testament from the sky and the rain and the wet nights with the wind blowing. It was easy speak in the towns with their justices and peelers to look after the law. With all their knowledge they did not know that Nell was no granddaughter of his but a daughter, bred out of a tinker's wife and him fifty. She was born from a game of cards. He could still recall the hand. Four aces and a king of diamonds. He had won her fairly.

Leibide Ludden shared his birth with Caesar. He was quarried out and never came through flesh. He had a big head with rolling eyes, which could not lock firmly on any object. He was awkward and ungainly and fond of the nipple. He drank and rolled easily into sleep leaving his body to the slow rhythm of vegetating.

Breast feeding over four years made him dependent and complacent. The world was no bigger than the fields about the house, the manure heap against the byre window, the slow movement of cows coming through the miry gate from the field, the rattle of cart wheels, an ass braying, a caller now and then with a bagful of stories. He wanted no more.

His grandfather died off. He was left with his mother in the house. He missed the old grandfather with his abusive tongue, his threatening stick. Half the population of the world was buried the day of the funeral. It was a sad shamble of burial, the coffin sticking out from behind the horse cart, a neighbour or two. He was only half-certain of what was happening. He remembered him lying in the soft silk of the ornamented packing case. He tried to shake him awake but there was no response from the stiff expression, only copper pennies over eyes. The grandfather's hands, forced into a posture of reverence, had yellowy dungrot about them.

He grew to manhood illiterate. He could neither reckon nor cipher. There were no niggling doubts. His knowledge lay within the limits of the farm; pig feeding, potato setting and digging, forking dung into a barrow and carrying it trailing to the garden patch; a knowledge of the four seasons, cutting shiny sods of turf from a bank, setting them to dry in the wind, stacking them and drawing them home. He could kill and salt a pig, hang bacon from the rafter where it browned under billowing smoke.

Leibide Ludden he was called and he had no schooling. No great brain grew inside his great head, or maybe there did but it was spongy loose, with no tense grip on knowledge. But he wanted no great knowledge about the farm. His mother did his thinking for him and there was no need to agitate his mind over yesterday or tomorrow.

He stood six feet seven in his stockinged feet and carried eighteen stone. He had not much to say to anybody, but people tapped their heads when they talked about him and said that there was no accounting for what he might do if he were stirred to anger. In general he was left to his ways, and the foul tongue of his mother kept him from harm.

He was a silent man in a grey, wet landscape, moved neither by great love nor great anger. He had a great fear of people, running to hide in the hayshed whenever a stranger came up the knobby road.

His life was secure. Humpy wet hills, a grey sky, a ribbon of road running aimlessly across the hills, a clump of frightened trees humping their backs to the scourging winds, the abstract shapes of exposed rocks filled his mind. Time had neither function nor termination. A man was alive and likely to live nearly for ever. His mother would live for ever. She was too independent to die. The farm house would stand the batter of wind and rain.

Nature renewed itself. Each year he set slits in spring and had potatoes by the end of summer. Time was easy.

But Big Nell was growing old and sagging. Her face was yellow and dry and ploughed. Arthritis twisted her finger joints into useless claws. She hobbled about the house on a crutch bawling orders at Leibide, tasking him in Irish and English. In old age she became religious, perhaps in order to atone for her sins, perhaps because she was lonely. The company of an idiot son forced her to surround herself with temperate saints. On the mantlepiece stood small pictures of the Sacred Heart, Saint Francis and Saint Brigid. Here and there about the house were medals and bottles of holy water to protect floor, hearth, thatch, eggs, milk and the plough-share from the attacks of the demons. The small farm on the hill was a theological battleground taken and retaken by the powers of good and the powers of evil. They were populated days when saints and demons lurked everywhere.

—Down on your knees, lad, she would say to Leibide, and we'll pray to the saints for all the departed souls waiting at the iron doors of Purgatory. Tonight if you keep your eye to the sky you might see a star falling which is a sign that some soul has been released.

Down he would go on his knees praying out loud and hard, keeping an eye out the window on the stars trying to prise them with prayers from the walls of heaven.

—I'm after knocking one off, he might roar, it fell into the lake.

—Good lad, she encouraged.

Some nights he often shook three stars from the branches of the sky. There were more dead than living, he thought to himself. His mother's mind stretched back to relations in America, England and Australia who had departed for the great unknown. He must have roared a hundred amens heavenwards every night.

A bad winter was the cause of her death. So they said, cluttered together in the wake house, the wind going in a hollow whistle up the chimney.

She resisted hard when the time came. She tossed in the bed, froth at the mouth, trying to untangle herself from the net of fate. A crowd stood above the tournament of death, looking down at the struggle. She lay alone in the bed, the poor powers of soul and body drawn up in combat. She snapped breath into her lungs, with wide horse-nostrils. She arched up in pain, dropped back dead. The warm sweat turned cold.

Leibide did not know she was dead. The crowd seemed to turn hostile. Someone moved toward him with an extended hand. —I'm sorry for your troubles.

—Keep away from me. I have no troubles. You want to take me away. I'll put me fist through the head of any man that touches me.

—Your mother is dead, the priest said.

—She's not, he told them, she's asleep. She always has that sour auld look on her puss when she's asleep. Wait until you hear her snoring in a minute or two. Then you'll know.

He looked down at the corpse, waiting for it to snore. Surely his mother would not let him down.

—What she needs is a bit of shaking and she'll be as right as rain, he told them.

He took his mother by the shoulders and shook her.

—Wake up, mother. 'Tis no time of the day to be sleeping and potatoes to be boiled and hens fed.

The head tossed limply like the head of a Martin de Porres statue on a mission box. No, it was not his mother he was shaking but a shrivelled wax dummy. The crowd were pulling at his shoulders, crying out at the desecration, the sounds of their voices breaking in small waves on his ears.

—Have you no respect for your mother? Let her soul rest in peace will you? She is gone now and there is no coming back.

He let his mother's corpse fall from his arms. There was nothing he could do now. He went down to the kitchen and sat mute in a rope chair, and bent his head in sadness. He was as desolate as the dry heather on the hill, or the cold cow shed, wet all winter with yellow dung slime, or the wind tearing on the bushes of a winter night.

In the wake house the dishevelled corpse was placed in a pious, defeated position. Death hardened the mould. A black worn beads tangled the fingers.

It did not concern Leibide. His mother was dead. No shaking or shouting could change the bleak fact. Take her away and bury her where they wished. Heel the coffin into a bog hole. He listened to the gurgle of black water about the sides and over the silver plate of the coffin. Then his imagination rejected the image. Perhaps a place among the slanted crosses, puffy moss growths, mouldering walls, would be the only place she would be happy. She would be away from her own in a bog hole, lonely and wet until the day she resurrected. And then when the trumpet sounded she would have to stray across the bogs to the consorting place alone, instead of being with others. And not having company, she could easily get lost and be left on the bleak earth alone.

They buried his mother on a Saturday morning against a dark charged sky. Rain was trailing tails when they left the mound of wet earth in the cemetery. Leibide plodded through hoof-puddles to Mickelmas Mac Lir's pub in the market place.

The ropes of rain twisted about the weighing scales in the market square. It was dark and dismal and dour outside. Men huddled under ass carts, or dragged potato bags to the weighing scales. Leibide took a pint of porter and went to the window and looked out, lost, life cracked.

Through the huddle of carts, careless and easy as a summer wind, came Kelly, and into the focus of Leibide's eyes.

He was tall, red haired, proportionately built, indifferent to the grey rain of the day.

CHAPTER TEN

Kelly walked across the market square and came into the bar. He had walked fifteen miles through a countryside as bare as a skeleton's bones from the edge of the sea. The tormented sky, the cry of the torn wind, the amplified sound of swollen streams shredded, sang in his mind.

He had spent a month on Duvillaun Mor island, living off goat flesh, seagulls' eggs, fish. He had dived each morning from the high cliffs into the sea and swam with seals learning their ways. He discovered the old ships lying with broken backs in fields of seaweed and carried away the gold from the chests and the pockets of dead sea captains.

On the grim island he rested in a rush hut, his strength growing.

They looked up from the thick gluey pints and wondered where he had come from, where his way was leading him.

—A pint, he called, and let it rest.

He shelved his back into the counter with his elbows. He looked at the funeral figures, the jobbers, the tinkers, all under the old beams of the Spanish Ship.

—A sad bunch of fools, he remarked to Mickelmas Mac Lir, the grandson of the proprietress, who lay in bed on the upper deck somewhere.

—Now, sir, if I were you I'd keep remarks of that nature to myself. You are in an angry place if tempers get aroused.

—Is it a wedding or a wake or bad weather? he asked.

—A lot of knotted reasons, the bad weather, the temper of Foxy Halligan who has come down to Belmullet after a sailor called Caoc Ainsworth, who did him out of a hundred pounds.

——That's Foxy Halligan, the Prince of the Tinkers? Kelly asked.

——The very same. A wicked, sullen man, and every one of the tribe with him.

——I've heard of him, Kelly said.

——And then we had a burial this morning. They have just finished shovelling clay over the remains of Big Nell Ludden. That's her lad over there. A strange fellow not to get tangled with either. He's the strongest man in the parish if you were to cross him. But he's simple and does not know greatly what has happened to him.

Kelly pivoted his fine head over towards Leibide, humped over a black drink, his brow dark.

——You're not afraid of the damp. Them clothes of yours are ringing bad, and it's foul for this time of year, Mickelmas Mac Lir said.

Kelly's clothes were steaming up, drying out.

——It's equal. No great harm will come out of it.

He took his pint, clattering small money onto the counter, clawed up his drink and walked over to Leibide.

——I'm sorry for your troubles, he said, settling beside Leibide.

——Me troubles?

——You're after burying your mother.

——Oh faith I didn't. I left that to Griffin the undertaker. I only looked on. I would have kept her about the house a while more, but the priest and doctor wouldn't hear of it. It's a terrible loss surely. It was a great thing having her about the house and never to worry about the drop of tea or the boiled meat and potatoes. God I haven't had a bit of decent food inside me mouth since she went away. 'Tis a terrible thing to think of me up there looking up at the mantlepiece on a winter's night at the holy pictures and statues, and devil a one to talk to but the old cat and me listening to the crickets at the back of the hob. 'Tis a fierce thing because the equal to her was not to be found. What they say about her is black. They take away her character and mine. I heard them, and me coming out of the graveyard. It will be lonely now because it takes a long time to learn how to talk to somebody and it is not everyone you can talk to.

He bent down over his drink, having said his long sentences. He locked his hand round the drink and took a mouthful. Silence thickened about him. Leibide, leaving down his pint, locked his thoughts between hinged fingers and crushed them. Kelly looked at the spread of his back, the black trail of coat, tight and smouldering damp. It heaved over sadness.

——Take it easy now and have another mouthful, Kelly said, patting the globe of his back, it's something that every man who ever lived had to face, and all the doctors from here to China couldn't do anything about it.

——Where's China? Leibide asked.

——A fair distance from here. Beyond Mullingar.

——That's a great stretch. As far as the stars at night when the winter is in the ground and me trying to bury myself under blankets. It's always cold up at the house in winter. No trees to hold off the rain.

——What will you do now?

——Well to tell the truth it didn't enter my head in any way. I could live out of the farm and the bog. Are you a farmer yourself? he asked.

——No.

——Or a cattle jobber?

——No.

His mind had no other alternatives. There was a gap in his talk.

——I'm a travelling man, you might say, going from place to place, with no town or village particularly in mind.

——It's an easy life.

——It's better than being planted in the one place all the time.

——I'd love to go with you. I often wondered what was beyond the hills. And going all day with no botheration in my head.

——You can come if you wish.

——It's a great temptation. Something I would have to give great consideration to.

——Fall in with me and share my adventures.

——I will. What will I call you?

——Kelly.

——Kelly.

——Will we travel far?

——There is no end to the roads in Ireland and you couldn't count the stopping places.

——I'm sure there is a lot to see.

——A different wonder every day.

Leibide stopped talking. Then he considered, a little consoled after burying his mother, Big Nell.

To Faustus MacGinty the square looked half a mile across and marshy. It must be near the end of the world. Further on somewhere there must be a battlement of cliff, and beyond that water. He was wet, coughing, fever burning in his small frame. He coughed, pain raking his lungs like a harrow. He wished he were rid of it, beyond the cope of grey sky.

The three feet of him shuffled across the square between bags of potatoes, creels, bound cabbage plants, cattle towering like elephants. Stars wheeling inside his head, struggling with their orbits. He held his head, bounding it against an explosion. He reeled down passages and arrived at the doors of the Spanish Ship. He stood inside the door. He looked up at the men drinking; they looked down at him. They had never seen the likes of it before. Faustus MacGinty saw only eyes. The eyes of cut-throats, jobbers, tinkers, tricksters, farmers.

Foxy Halligan roared in laughter.

——Look at the little leprechaun of a man, he told them. He cracked their shell of wonder.

——He must have shrunk in the rain, he added.

——Not at all, six-eighths of him ran down the leg of his father's trousers, Angel said.

Foxy Halligan nearly fell from his stool at the remark. Porter spewed out through his nostrils and mouth and nearly choked him. Tears ran down from his eyes and he slobbered them across his cheeks with the sleeve of his coat.

——You wouldn't see the likes of him in a circus, he told the Halligan clan.

——Maybe he's one of the small people, Angel Halligan said. He's surely carrying some devilment in them eyes of his. Don't let him hold you in the stare of his eyes. They're looking east and west, two different ways, a thing unheard of.

—He's not normal at all, Foxy said, come over till we have a look.

They circled around Faustus MacGinty, went on their knees, a bit in wonder, a bit in fear and bound by the twine of superstition. They looked firmly at the wonder. Sure enough the two eyes were rolling around in two different directions.

—There is no knowing where he might have come from, Casta Halligan said.

—He could have been washed ashore from an African boat. He may be the eighth wonder of the world. He's no dwarf like Hegarty the Hunchback, who's only half a man with a man's width, the fellow that married the Regan one with the lame step, Angel said, looking for comparison.

—He's a class apart sure enough, like a child's shoe made from leather and nails, Casta said.

Faustus looked at the valley of drunk, monstrous faces walling out the world. They were big and ugly, enlarged by a lens of fear. He noticed the slobber on their faces, the dirty skin, and the rime of beard stubble, bull-baiters, cock-fighters.

Behind them were men of middle character, afraid of being good or bad, and filling up space. Faustus did not feel the wet sweat through his clothes, only the fear, the fear of a small animal in a slaughter house.

Foxy Halligan's hungry bitch, the mix of a thousand mongrels, nosed in through the wall and stuck her head into the ring. —After him, Stocker, Foxy encouraged.

She was in the ring now, slyly circling, cute eyes waiting to jump. The crowd watched mute. She snarled and snapped at him. Faustus jumped back to the wall, edged from knee to knee, watching at the immoral eyes of the dog almost even with his. She sprang again. He screeched in his castrated voice. But she stood back taking her time, sensing the encouragement of the crowd. Then she jumped and savaged his arm, dragging him to the ground, tearing at him, like she would tear and worry a rabbit. She dragged him behind her about the arena, the crowd cheering, knowing now that the little man was mortal, bearing no great power in his size. She would have mangled him, but Foxy Halligan caught him by the leg and tugged him away, held him by the leg above her. Faustus MacGinty looked at the world upside down, dangling. He could have been in hell, the sport of whirlwind and fire, bundled and tossed by a chaotic whim.

He was so small and removed from normal size that no one would worry about killing him and throwing him in a ditch. The ravens would eat him, the hawk carry him up to the cliffs in her claws. There was joy too in looking at him shrivel with fear, every nerve in his body mad to be preserved. Beating him to pulp and mashing him in with turnips would be as enjoyable as raping the parson's daughter, the one with the grand airs. Maybe let him run from a pen at a day's coursing and watch the greyhounds break his back.

Not that one by one some of them were not decent men. They went to Mass on Sunday and took their hats off to the priest. A few of them would die for Ireland if the call went out, and one or two of their fathers had. There is a cross to one of them in the place where he died and an inscription in Irish. Horsemen and assmen throw a cold eye on it, going home from fairs or agricultural functions, and pass by, or maybe come down for a prayer and then turn to the ditch for a piss. There was that class of man among them.

This was only a black spasm of unreason, a cistern, suppurating for a while, throwing up sullen bile, raw hate; the wild urge on a sodden day to join in a ritual of butchery and blood. A twist in the soul of the Celtic race.

Foxy Halligan put Faustus MacGinty on the counter and looked at him.

——I wonder if he has any balls? he asked.

——Begob, there is no man born who hasn't, said Casta.

——How do you know? How many pairs of balls have you ever seen?

——Me own and a few others.

——Well that doesn't mean there aren't elephants in Africa.

——I never thought of it like that.

——That's why you're the idiot you are.

—Well if he hasn't, find out.

—I'm going to.

They discovered one.

—Only one. The size of a nut. You couldn't do much damage with that. No wonder he is only the size he is. Now how would you let a man like that up and down the roads of Ireland? We'd have a race of small men in a generation and couldn't go to war, Foxy argued.

—It would mean that they would eat less and wear less. It might save an awful lot of problems, Angel told him.

—What do you say, lads, if I cut it out? It will save him carrying weight.

He took a long jack-knife from his pocket and opened it slowly, an eye closed and nodding his head. They were tittering and waiting. Faustus MacGinty began to cry like a cornered rabbit, with an irrational, sad cry.

—Come over here to me. There's a good edge on the knife and before you can say 'God save the Queen', we'll have the job done.

—Hold it, a rough voice said from the window. It was harsh like a saw scraping stone. They looked down through the filtered, grey light at Kelly, his shirt open, his chest matted with red hair. Behind him stood Leibide Ludden, looking over his shoulder. Leibide derived great strength from this man Kelly who did not seem to give a damn for wind, rain or any man.

—And who would you be with your thatch of red hair and big words in your gob? Foxy Halligan asked.

—You wouldn't be Foxy Halligan by any chance? Kelly asked.

—You heard of me?

—Sort of.

—Well then I'm a man to keep away from, particularly when I'm in a temper.

—You gap toothed, foul mouthed, low bred bastard, I'll give you, your idiot of a brother, your father, and whatever other weeds of your kind are here, five minutes to leave the place before I claw the manhood out of you with the nails of my fingers.

—Move, Foxy Halligan. When Kelly means move he

means take to the air and you better be scurrying off, Leibide Ludden said.

—Two idiots instead of one, Foxy Halligan said.

—Is your hearing faulty or do you want me to say it again? Kelly called, heat coming into his body.

—You are a brave one, very free with your words as if you had money to spend, Foxy said.

—I'm going to stand by what I say.

The crowd stood aside and formed into a pool about the two fighters.

—Keep away from me or I'll draw blood, Foxy Halligan warned, crouching down into a springing position.

—I'll cut the collops out of you with this weapon.

—So you say, Kelly said, turning up the sleeves of his shirt, following the cunning eyes. I'll tear you asunder, rip the skin off your bones and twist them around your thick neck. Do you hear me? roared Kelly.

—I hear you and I'll shove every word from your mouth a yard back your gullet.

They circled about, kneading the space between them.

—In at him, Foxy. Kick the tools off him, the father encouraged, stamping the ground impatiently with his knobbly blackthorn stick.

Foxy sprang inwards, stabbing with his knife, searing Kelly's arm, blood running. Rage ran through Kelly.

—You have him, Foxy. Give it to him where he feels it most, we'll feed him to the dogs.

Kelly's eyes were burning red. He heard Tarbh roaring from outside the crowd. —What are you waiting for, you idiot. Do you think I can spend the whole night sitting in this barn looking at you dance? Get in and work him over.

Foxy hurled himself at Kelly, curling down the knife at Kelly's back. Kelly stood aside, his knee up to meet teeth and jaw. Bones snapped and there was a shower of teeth. Foxy spat them out and came charging back. Kelly pounded his nose flat, milling the soft bone into flour. He was on the top of Foxy now, his fingers on his throat screwing his flesh, choking off the air. Foxy's eyes were rolling.

Angel Halligan brought down the knob of the blackthorn stick on the back of Kelly's skull, cracking the bone. He was drawing up for another wallop when he was heaved off the floor, pulled onto the counter and smashed down the far side with a crack from Leibide Ludden's fist.

—Leave Kelly alone. It's a fair fight, Leibide said.

Angel on hunkers crawled towards the door. Leibide ran after him and booted him out on the cheeks of his backside into the street.

Kelly bent down and caught Foxy Halligan by the danglers and the hair of the head.

—Oooooooo Aaaaaaaa Uuuuuuuu Iiiiiii Eeeeee, vowelled Foxy in pain.

Kelly carried him to the door and, swinging him three times, threw him into a cart of squealing bonhams. Kelly, his eye shooting meteors, looked at the remnants of the tribe in corners and under the table. He tore after them with his boot kicking flesh and bone until they were out in the square and running in the direction of the different winds like a startled huddle of crows.

—I'll get even with you, if it's the last thing I do on this earth. I'll get even with you, Foxy roared from among the bonhams.

There were only four of them left in the bar; Kelly, bleeding, blazing-eyed; Leibide, satisfaction on his gob; Faustus MacGinty, and Mickelmas Mac Lir, the grandson of the woman who owned the pub.

Kelly looked up at Tarbh, guffawing with laughter.

—You're a good one in a scrap, me old flower, and I could let you out any day. That was a fair grip you got on Foxy Halligan, but beware of him. He's black and twisted like the blackthorn. And one thing I must tell you. You are mortal. Before I go I also must tell you that you want a horse. You'll find one out in the Craoisleach bog on the way down to Sleas under Gorta hill. He's the best there is in Ireland for speed and agility. He's called Lubach Caol and a great lepper.

Tarbh faded out through the black wall, bringing the armchair with him, like the ghost of Hamlet's father. None but Kelly had heard or seen him.

Mickelmas Mac Lir studied the damage. Better he thought the misty, narrow streets of Prague. Better the comforts of a civilized man. Better mists rolling through a web of streets at night, gas bulbs blooming, houses leaning with ears listening, than this land of Erris.

The Irish had mad humours. Savage and raw as stone, wet as turf, stupid as the eternal mists. This was the uncertain edge of Europe. Sea wreckage they were, driftwood from the ocean.

Kelly looked at the battleground.

—How much? he asked.

—Forty sovereigns, Mickelmas Mac Lir answered, doubling the charge.

—Take it from these, and he skittered gold across the counter, merry, twinkling.

—Roman? Mickelmas asked.

—No, Kelly said.

—Greek? Mickelmas inquired.

—No. Spanish.

Mickelmas bit at the substance of the coins. Weighed them on his hand.

—Where did they come from?

—The pockets of rotted sea captains at the bottom of the sea.

Mickelmas fingered through his money box.

—Change, he said, giving back five sovereigns.

—Add fifty more and we're right, Kelly said.

Mickelmas ripped up a floor board, pulled up silver and gold coins and handed them over to Kelly. Kelly gave him back the Arabic and Chinese pieces.

—Odd type of money for these parts, Kelly said.

—We have sinister callers, Mickelmas replied.

—These coins are a queer age, Kelly told him.

—'Tis an odd place, Mickelmas shrugged.

Faustus MacGinty still stood on the counter, dragging his mad army of nerves into order.

—Button your trousers, Kelly ordered, you'll get a cold in your bollocks if you are not careful.

—I'll button them for him, Kelly. His hand is dead, Leibide said.

He did. Then he took Faustus under the crook of his arm and carried him over to the fire. The two of them bound his bleeding arm in linen and slung it on sailcloth. They gathered armchairs around the fire.

——Mac Lir, Kelly roared, bolt the doors against the night. Bring a creel of turf in from the stack. Boil all the cabbage and bacon you have in the house and call out when they are ready. We're staying the night.

——We have only two beds, sir. One for me and one for me grandmother and she's close on a hundred and twenty.

——How does she manage to keep alive?

——On kippers and the drop of porter. On kippers and the drop of porter.

——The three of us will sleep with your grandmother, if you have no objections.

——God almighty, you couldn't do that. It would be a scandal broadcast among the nine hills of the eight parishes.

——You sleep with her then.

——That would be worse still, for I'd be like Oedipus in the tale. It's hunger eats me, Mickelmas said.

——'Tis not starving it you are, Kelly said.

——It would be against all laws to give in to my queer thoughts, Mickelmas said.

——What do you know about law? Faustus asked.

——Only what I heard. Only what I read in the pamphlets.

——There is only good and evil. Do good, don't do evil. But who is to say what good is and what evil is? Faustus told him.

——You are playing at words now like the men in the law-courts. 'Tis too much for my mind. I'll go out and get a settle bed from the back and I'll sleep in the parlour. I'll have no queer practices under this roof.

——Each man to his own evil and his own good, Faustus said.

——You're at it again, Mickelmas said, and off he went to put down the pots of bacon and cabbage and dig new potatoes by paraffin light.

Night had come. It was comfortable under the heavy roof and the tarred beams. The three were silent, listening to the roar of the fire, the hollow surf-boom of wind running up the flue. They felt welded. Odd men against the world, Kelly now the leader.

——Where do we go from here? Leibide asked.

——We'll rest here awhile. Then we'll take whatever particular road strikes our fancy. We'll go up and down the country, to patterns, fairs, wakes, weddings, funerals.

——It looks a grand idea, Kelly, Leibide said.

——I suppose it is. Better than being anchored in one place.

——And you know, Kelly, the story of what you did today will go in front of us. For you did something that no other man could do. You chased the Halligans out of a public house, as if they were a crowd of midges.

——They were easy handled.

Kelly turned to Faustus.

——Who are you and what's your name?

——MacGinty. Faustus MacGinty. A Munster man going from grave slab to grave slab writing down Latin inscriptions.

——It's a queer way of making a living.

——I could be shaving corpses, Faustus said, offering an alternative.

——Well you could.

——But sure I'll go with you. You did a great deed today and I'm more than thankful.

When Mac Lir had the potatoes boiling, he served the three drinks, a pint for Kelly and Leibide, a thimble of whiskey for Faustus. He had never taken it before. Drink was a new experience to him. His senses had almost dried up with years of reading and vicarious experience. He rolled the drops on his tongue, happy with the existence of taste in his mouth. They sat on after Mac Lir had gone to bed. In the silence they were making plans, going down roads. Leibide, for the moment, had forgotten that he had buried his mother.

——We'll go to bed, men, Kelly ordered after he had drunk a half barrel of porter, which he had heaved up on the table beside him. He felt warm in his stomach.

——Take Faustus upstairs and warm the bed for me, Kelly told Leibide.

——Right you be, Kelly.

And he took Faustus under his arm and climbed up the stairs to the second storey.

Kelly went outside the front door for a piss. It was a black night. He pissed for half an hour, keeping his hands in his pockets and whistling because he was a god.

CHAPTER ELEVEN

The rain had thinned in the morning. Kelly, Faustus MacGinty, Leibide Ludden looked from the second storey window of the Spanish Ship over the slut of village. A street of low houses, staggered roofs and windows like old faded faces. At one end the blunt tower of Protestant steeple, yew trees, soldiering the edge of the cemetery, a sparse crop of crosses. Beyond it the rectory, red sandstone walls; grey slates, French windows onto a green lawn and protected roses.

The Catholic church was built on a hump of hill, beside a ruin, coated with ivy, the graveyard thick with dead; crosses and standing slabs in the rich crop of coarse grass.

——'Tis no day for any type of work, complained Leibide, ——we might as well go back to bed while the sheets are warm and wait for tomorrow. Something might turn up.

He turned towards the bed but Kelly caught him by the hasp of the trousers.

——Not now. We have to look for a horse to carry us from place to place and then we'll be right, Kelly told him.

——Where will you get a horse at this time of day? Leibide asked.

——Out near Sleas in Craoisleach Bog, Kelly told him.

——But Craoisleach Bog stretches eight miles between mountains and no horse would go into it with bog holes. A fellow coming from Crossmolina one night fell into a bog hole and was never heard of since, Leibide told him.

——Well there's a horse grazing out there and we must go out and find him, Kelly said.

—Leave him where he is. Me head is heavy after yesterday. We'll get back into bed, Leibide pleaded.

The three went back into bed.

Mickelmas Mac Lir's grandmother, carrying lightly her hundred and twenty years, was lying in the storey above them. It was hard to tell whether she was a man or woman with a senile goatee of grey wisps under her chin. Loose, freckled, furrowed skinface, patched white, blotched like leprosy, her pipe of a gullet visible under yellow wrinkled skin. She had no earthly intention of dying. Why should she and the world to live for? She owned fifty acres from the bed. And then there was con acre and two thousand sheep on the mountain. And then there was an acre here and an acre there on the nine hills of the eight parishes. She had an idiot of a grandson who ran the pub. Not that he was her grandson. There was no line in the family. He was a bastard dropped by a Keegan girl she had taken in forty-five years ago.

She had the memory of more than a century at the back of her head; a hundred and eighteen years in fact, each year like a field which gave a good or bad yield depending on the circumstances of peace or war. She often lamented that the last ninety years of her life had been spent at the end of Europe. She knew a lot of men and a lot of places in her day. Mixed images rising from her mind. Of nightrides in carriages, a white horse carrying her between the trees of a park, crooked streets in cities and narrow openings into sinister yards, hay in her skirts, bare floors, sailors and boatmen and mixed words and languages, wine in better times, fruit, the uniforms and boots of soldiers on the floor. A fat king carrying her into a feast and her lying naked on a tray. A painter, easel, canvas, her opulent body spread across the silk coverlet of a bed, backside up. The dry wind of the desert, day travel under the hot sun, a cool fountain and cool marble under her back. His black skin and matted hair above her.

A bad winter at sea brought her to Belmullet. The ship torn on the rocks on her way to America, after the new gold. Two survivors, herself and Manaman Mac Lir. A black night on the strand, the claws of the sea grabbing at them. Manaman dragged her from its maw; they survived and mated. The gold sown in her corset set them up. He followed a military call to change geography at the end of the world. There was a drawing of him in foolish battle dress on the wall, serious and grim with a handlebar moustache. A letter or two from a war front. She had almost forgotten him for he had spent too many years away from her bed.

She knew them all. The rich with their bags of gold, the beggar that wanted a toss for twopence. The same hunger in the stiff gut. Mickelmas told her about Kelly next morning when he brought her up her pint of porter and kippers.

—One of them by the name of Kelly is a red hairy man, strong as Matt McGee and his father. I could swear he grew bigger the more he got angry and the quare eye he has was shot with red, like a fire kindled in Hell.

—Bring him up until I get a look at him. It's a long time since my eyes rested on a fine looking man.

There was a randy look in her eyes.

—Is it more porter you're after?

—No. Send up Kelly.

—I don't know if I should be the one to obtrude on the mighty gentleman, carrying with him as he does and it easily stirred a temper that scattered Foxy Halligan and his breed across half the bogs of Mayo, not knowing as we don't which of them is dead or living.

—Stop your mouth with your long litany of destruction. You're assaulting me eardrums. When you go downstairs put on all the bacon and cabbage you've got and set them to boil in the grate here, she ordered.

—You couldn't eat bacon and cabbage, Mickelmas told her.

—What do you know what I'll be ready for when I've finished with great exercise, she said.

—Now the only exercise you can get in that bed is fart and empty your scowery old bowels.

—I'll take the stick to you now if I hear any more from you and I'll raise welts on your back that you can sow potatoes in. Bring up an ass load of turf and throw it in the fire.

There was a slobbery look of ignorance on his face, so he followed her orders. He carted up bales of turf, puffing, panting, complaining. The old one was taking leave of her senses, he thought.

—Have you the cabbage on? she asked.

—Sure I haven't eight pair of hands like the Vasudhara out of Ancient India, he said.

—None of your knowledgeable chat. Where did you hear about her? she asked.

—An Indian that called one night on his way to Achill, he said.

—Is me chamber pot empty? she asked.

—It is. Don't rush me with all the orders. It ravels me mind.

—Now before you go I want you to do something and follow the instructions I give you very carefully.

She drew a warm key from between her leathery dugs.

—Did you ever hear of the African Box?

—The Dirty Box of Africa you mean?

—That's right, she said.

—Sure they talk about it, but it is only a queer twisted action in their heads, he told her.

—It might be more than that, Mickelmas. Pull across the long curtain at the end of the room.

The curtain had stood there like a frontier to a strange country for ninety years, covering the mysteries of the Dirty Black Box of Africa. People said it had come from a wrecked Phoenician ship; that it was not a box but a room; that it was as broad as it was long; that it carried all the sun-tanned evil of Africa in it. Others said that it was brought by a man from Algiers who came one summer evening in across the molten twilight waters of the bay and him sashed in silks and gold, a turban on his head, the toes of his shoes cocked up like the shoes of leprechauns. Dark and brown women with naked breasts about him that drove the parish half-mad with southern lust for months. That it turned men's heads and that they didn't dig potatoes or cut hay that summer, and winter found them hungry. They had the rumour that even to this day there are Keegans and Crishams and Morahans and Flahertys walking over North Africa, riding camels, that never saw their fathers.

She remembered the man from Africa. He had tracked

her down, tackled his ships and came after her. Black slaves, many of whom died of the whooping cough and were buried outside Leitir cemetery, carried the box as big as a room up the street from the pier. They had taken the slates off the roof and put the box at the end of the bedroom and then put the roof back again. So the story goes and it goes further. He locked himself in the room with her for all the summer months. They still talk of the strange music which came from the room, of the golden laughter, of the screams of angers, the screeches, ecstasy, the lash and snap of whips, the noise of pursuit, the house shaking, mortar falling from walls and ceiling, the foundations shaking until they thought a randy devil was loose in the upper storey. Two months later, autumn nearly dead, the man from Africa was carried from the room, his silks in shreds, grey-haired and old, a mad, high glaze of pleasure on his staring eyes. He looked eighty; that old. He never spoke. They carried him to the ship, raised the sails of silk and departed.

Mickelmas Mac Lir's grandmother, knacker yard material, old bones over dry marrow, blotched, chappy skin over old lime bones, knew the story of the black box, with burnished doors, a carved book of love. It had been crafted by Harein-El-Shadid over a period of forty years. He had carved it from cedar carried from Lebanon to Algiers. He was a skilled eunuch. Forty years in a spacious tower, standing above the desert and the sea he worked. They carried materials to him from about the Mediterranean; silk, copper, silver, gold. In the lower rooms of the tower a school of craftsmen worked under his direction. No one had ever seen the assembling of the room or its completion. Complete and complicated, it stood and him old. Half his life he had spent mastering his craft and half his life he had spent building a single object from the resources of the world. And so it was ready for the young sultan. The eyes of Harein-El-Shadid were gouged out, his tongue was cut and he was left to roam the bazaars writing his strange story on dust and sand. She knew it all from behind rheumy eyes. The memory did not stir her worn body. There had been too much burning, too much frenzy. But still a small spark lay in the ashes.

—Did you pull across the curtain? she asked.

—No. I'm afraid to. I always wondered what was in here.

—Well, pull across the curtain and see.

Mickelmas opened the long mysterious curtain which had concealed the lower end of the room for nearly ninety years. It was of black wood, dark as night, heavy and embossed, figures excavated out of four inches of timber. Micklemas Mac Lir never saw the likes of it for pictures before. Nothing that had ever run into his mind and his desires hot was like it. He dug his fingers into the excavated world, running them over bodies and places and sacred woods. Fine finished women, with hard polished bodies, stiffened into a wild pose, randy and loving for eternity. And then the bubby man under the tree swilling wine, bleary eyed and no conscience trouble. Mickelmas probed his pendulous stomach, an eternal cask of wine. He screwed his thumb into the tunnel of navel. The button might snap and the belly bounce free and wobble, turning the wine sour, he thought. He leered from the arm rest of root, inviting celebates under the jovial branches.

A rafty shell settled on a sea, a hair blown woman, with unsecular flesh on her opulent body, looked with an uncommitted expression on the world. The shell was a boat womb. And beyond all the dominant figures, in landscapes he saw the fine lines of other worlds. The door was big enough to be the doorway of a low cathedral. It had strong proportions. Panels ran along the sides, picturing miniature worlds, perfect and exact. It was like looking down on a scene from a round tower.

His blood was frothing with head; he leaped about like an unsatiated libertine, drinking the voluptuous experiences indiscriminately. His head was giddy.

—Call Kelly, his grandmother roared from the bed.

He did not heed. He ran from the room, down the stairs, out into the guttery street, strong as a horse. He jumped the high walls about the parson's garden, ran along the path breaking the roses, and up the stairs where the parson's daughter was lying in bed eating toast. She screamed when she saw the guns of war on her frontier, screamed at the invasion, protested, cried. No avail. Her cities were destroyed,

her wheat fields scorched by licking fire, her streams
muddied, her woods felled, her cattle slaughtered, spitted,
eaten. Her dykes finally broken.

They led him away; half-idiot, blank faced, slobbering
foam at the mouth. It was over like a flash. God-fallen, they
led him away, bound him with ropes and brought him to the
asylum in Castlebar. And from there started the legend of the
Dirty Dark Box of Africa.

The grandmother, deserted, took a small phial from under
her pillow, rich with arabesques of Islam. She broke the
nipple with her nail and drank the green drops. It drained
away the corrosion of time, and ran into the marrowbone
like sweet resin. Honey across her flesh, ointment and oil. It
called her bones and muscles and ligaments to life. It was a
rich, unmonastic liquid. Life pounded through the rooms of
her body. Flesh bloomed with blood, old skin scales peeled
away. New skin creamed. Eyes cleared of ague, misery and
pain-twist. Her men had been too long at war; ninety years.
She was a city under siege for too long. Under perpetual grey
skies where bees never gathered honey. Where ugly hagged
winds waited, waited to keen death.

Now she was strong. She jumped free of the bed, tore the
dirty shift from her body, stood naked, splayed, brown
skinned, dark hair running on her back burnished like blue
Castile steel, and under her armpits matted and bushed,
and between her legs. She would have no clothes about her.
Let the air sweeten and fatten on her flesh. Let her comb
the ample pads of sensual flesh with preening fingers. Her
body a brown guitar, strung, toned, to be played. She went
to the door, pushed the navel of Bacchus, and the nipple of
Venus. A combination snapped together inside, humming
like an oiled and thoughtful mind. She stood before it
unfolding, hands on hips. The doors let out their light, their
perfume. It was as it had been when she had dragged her
sultan out, drugged, seventy years ago. It shone before her,
a neat intact place of pleasure. She rushed to a wardrobe and
searched for silk linen for her body, stockings, and the
dark satin dress. She looked down at the far end of the room.

—Damn that fellow, she said to herself, he forgot to put on
bacon and cabbage.

When she was ready she went to the door and called down.
——Kelly.

They heard the call.

——I didn't know there was a young female in the house, Kelly said.

——It's the old one, Leibide remarked.

——It couldn't be, said Faustus, that voice, judging from its quality, comes from Spain, like the bones of the dead sea captains.

——This is a house of unending surprises. I might as well go and investigate, for no man could resist a call like that, Kelly said.

——I suppose not, Leibide said.

——Come on, Kelly, the voice called again.

——I'm coming, he roared, will you give me time to find my directions.

Kelly made his way through the maze of the illogical inn. In a corner he found a Spanish iron-wrought gate, leading up twisting stairs. The old flint segments rang with the metal of his nailed boots.

——The place must be built around an old castle, he thought to himself. On he went, twisting up and away like a dancing mind.

——In here, Kelly. A call came from behind a door.

He pulled open the door and there she stood, in black lace and Spanish brocade. She looked at Kelly framed in the door, the wild red hair, the strange opal eye. The red trangle of bushy rust on his chest like a well cured goat skin. The legs firm under the toned trunk. He looked at her, white fire kindling in his opal eye, foddered by her sensual body. She winked at him, a dark mediterranean wink and walked into the black box padded with crimson. He followed her across the floor and into the room of thick, toe-high carpet.

——There are wonders and wonders and wonders, and I suppose I should have taken off me boots but I can't take my eyes off her, he thought.

The door swung closed behind them and snapped privacy on them. Guitar music started and she began to dance about him in love circles.

——I'll burn him to the ground, and he thinking that he is

champion who can fight any man who walks the roads, she thought to herself.

He stepped up beside her and joined in the dance.

——Where did you learn your Spanish dancing? she asked.

——From a spoiled priest who was in Salamanca for years, he said.

——You're not having me on?

——Sure as I'm doing my steps, it's true.

The pace of the music smartened.

He snapped an ivory comb from her hair and let it run.

He arched his body on toes like a grandee.

——Where in Hell did he come from? she wondered to herself.

His face sneered down at her. He danced, his shirt stripped from him, a patina of fine sweat on his skin. He undid her bodice and skirt. She was naked beside him but for her Spanish shoes and earrings. Now they held glasses of wine firmly in their hands and danced. She put it to her mouth and let it spill over sensual lips, down over the peninsulae of her breasts and trickle into the sacred wood. Kelly tongued it from her stiff nipples and off the fruits of her flesh.

——Are you sure you're from Mayo?

——Sure I'm from Mayo.

——And did you travel?

——Devil a bit, except in the books and the old tales that I heard around the fire at night.

——It's beyond understanding.

——There is many a thing beyond understanding if we knew the ins and outs of everything.

Kelly was now naked. She had never seen a body like it before. It was like a king's game preserve.

——Now, she said when the music had twisted the contours of the world. He took her by the black hair, bound it around his hand, put his free hand under her backside and carried her to the bed. They climbed through the six bright days of her body. Sword after sword of pleasure was stabbed into her. She rolled away from the enemy. He pursued her through the grass. He cut finely again. She moaned in pleasure, wondering would muscle melt from bone. Her flesh was honey.

——Where did he come from? He has been through this dance eight thousand and fifty times, she thought.

The music ended. The sea threw her on to the sand. She lay sea-wrecked.

——No knowing what damage he's doing or having done to him, Faustus said.

——Kelly can take care of himself. Didn't you see him handle half a field of tinkers. I'd bet me last shilling on him in an ass race across Curragh Strand.

——If my conjectures are correctly built on any knowledge I have, and it's not inconsiderable, Kelly should be well worn out by now.

——Like a bull.

——Like the bull and all other animals.

——Still and all, Kelly is in a class all his own.

——I know. I know. But I'm only saying.

The town went through another rainy night. It rattled on the roof and Leibide and Faustus in bed. They looked out the window in the morning. Thin, grey rain, like a ribby cow, ate the light of the sun. The dung on the square dissolved into green slime, trickled away. A door or two was opened, an ass brayed in a field. Crows swarmed and reswarmed in the trees over the Protestant graveyard.

——A place without event or happening, Leibide remarked.

——What do you want, asked Faustus, to go to China and eat rice?

——Where is China?

——A good distance east with a wall about it.

That satisfied Leibide.

When Kelly opened his eyes, the room had changed. The walls were hung with heavy tapestries, showing knights on prancing horses and ladies on amblers, deers caught in formal brambles. A troubadour among rose bushes in a walled garden played a lute. She sat demurely by a castle window, overlooking distances. Kelly lay on the bed, battle-tired, his linen armour stained.

——There are no end to wonders, he thought to himself.

——You are late, my lord, she said.

——And why shouldn't I be? I've come a long way. It's been a long journey, across deserts, through dark forests in the north. We were shipwrecked once.

——You thought of me.

——Sure if she's mad I might as well placate her, he thought to himself.

——Yes, Nightingale of Provence.

The words pleased her to no end.

——You have the nice way of putting things, Kelly, she said from the window.

——I say nothing that's not in my heart, he lied, and I'd swear that on a Paladin's sword.

——Will you play for me on the lute? she asked.

——Lute? he questioned himself, oh yes, the lute.

And he looked at the bulbous instrument like a sliced onion lying on a chair. He took the lute and played songs he had learned of Southern France, of Spain, Muslim songs, songs he had learned of Sicily.

Evening beyond the window, profiled her face. His voice was as soft as a Pasha's couch. He sang of walled gardens and roses. By twilight she was like wine in his mouth. They laboured gently together. When there was no wine left, Kelly fell asleep. She looked down on him. There was a malicious look of sensuality in her eyes. She would wear the strength out of him if it took her the eighty new years in her body.

Leibide Ludden had considered the music.

——I never knew that Kelly could play the fiddle. They're the queerest tunes it was ever me fortune to listen to and I have heard many a travelling fiddler.

——That's not a fiddle, Leibide, Faustus told him, I'd swear by all the books of Gregorian chant in the monasteries that he's playing a lute.

Leibide had nothing to say to that. They cocked their ears and listened. The lute music lasted a week; day in, day out; night in, night out.

——That's medieval French he's singing now, Faustus said, sitting up in bed one night.

——It's soft raimeis if you ask me anything. There is only one language and that's the one you're speaking, Leibide said, disturbed from his sleep. He pulled away the blanket from Faustus who was unaware of the cold. Leibide, feeling the mawclaw of hunger, took a pig's crubeen from a barrel by his bed, chewed on its succulent fat and threw the bone into a wooden bath.

Faustus followed the troubadour through Europe, through Spain, down into Sicily, over to Cyprus, into Jerusalem, on to Damascus. It satisfied all the directions of his mind.

Kelly slept and dreamed of meadows, thick with asphodel. Distant balalaika music stole across the pillow into his ears. It came across a wide river from a tavern. It was a Russian night with a polished moon; snow hard on banks; infinite spaces, dark clumps of resinous trees. The boat moved over ink waters to a huddle of hovels about the tavern. The music seduced his mind and built images in it. He opened his eyes. He stood at the door of a dark tavern. A large open fire spat blue flame.

She danced in the shadows, flared skirt, embroidered blouse. The music grew louder. Her blouse burst open, showing large heavy breasts, like swollen melons. His desires ran savage. He caught her from the swirling circle of music. She tore at his face, scraped sharp nails across his neck. He screamed in pain and released her. Gipsy wildness burned in her eyes. A dagger quivered in her hand. They faced one another across the floor, circling like cautious wolves. He lunged at her, a knife blade searing his chest, blood running through the matted hair. He pulled a fishing net from the ceiling, threw it on her body, caged her. He carried her to the table, tangled in the net. They ate each other's marrow.

The house rocked under them, mortar falling from the ceiling, old beams creaking. She was free, running. He caught her, locked her with his arms to a supporting beam, printing the roughness of the wood on her back.

——It's the end of the world, Leibide said, looking up at the groaning rafters, Kelly will be the death of us. I've never known the earth to shake under me like it, since the day they blasted the rocks in the quarry.

——It's a house of wonders, Faustus said.

Leibide prayed to his saints for the general stability of the world, dashing his rosary trimmings together into a compound prayer against natural disasters.

The village shook. A split appeared on Cnocan slope, a sow farrowed three calves, the parish priest's theology books toppled down on him in his sedate study.

She looked at the exhausted figure on the bed, her body tortured, threadbare, the phial empty. The silt of age was clogging the conduits of pleasure. She was out of place, out of time. She was beaten by the sprawled giant, she cursed her failing strength, pulling down the mansion of life about her. She took the wet flesh.

—Wake up, she called, time is running out.

—How do you mean?

—I can't tell you. Time runs out fast when you take pleasure.

—How much time has run on us?

—A month for you. Now I'm forty, soon I'll be fifty and then I'll be a hundred and twenty.

—That's some running.

—My own doing, she complained, looking at her dry skin.

—Tell me who you are, she croaked at sixty.

—One of the old gods, he started laughing, you coupled with a god, you old viper, thinking you'd suck me dry.

He jumped from the bed and shook her bones.

—Tell me all the rest before I shake you apart.

And he shook the old dry carcass.

—Run, she said, run fast and don't look back until you are up on Sliabh Gorta. Run before you burn with me, for I'm Hell-bound now, to pay hard to the great usurer himself. He'll be leering tonight and I can hear his laughter in my ears.

A pungent smoke of smouldering cedar wood filled the room. He threw her on the bed, grabbed his trousers and shirt and ran out of the room. He stopped a moment to put them on outside the door, ran down the winding stairs and into the bar.

Leibide sat at the table, drunk, empty porter barrels around him like the broken columns of a Greek temple.

——Hell for leather now to the hills or we'll be on our way to Hell, he told them.

——Hell? hiccuped Faustus, drunk.

——Yes.

——I'm afraid I can't agree with you. I have strong theological doubts about the existence of Hell under the following headings, Faustus splayed out the fingers of his right hand to hang his theological arguments on.

Kelly knew there was no talking to them. He had two idiots in tow. He pushed Faustus inside his shirt, put his arm around Leibide, headed across the square, down the road and up Sliabh Gorta. It was dark. He looked down towards the town.

The flames started up from the Spanish Ship. They hesitated at first, licked the roof, fed well. Soon the roof was on fire. It lit up the village. There was a commotion in the square, voices in confusion, figures running here, there and everywhere.

——Are we nearing the gates of Hell? Leibide asked.

——Faith we are. We should be there in ten minutes, if we're running on time, Kelly told him.

——I'm too young to go to Hell, Leibide said, I want to see a priest. I want to tell him I'm a bad man.

——I still think there is no Hell, Faustus said, sticking his head out through the neck of Kelly's shirt.

Explosions of airy lights patterned the sky. Finally there was a brilliant burst of light above the house. And there, from the blazing roof of the house, emerged Mickelmas Mac Lir's grandmother, riding the devil's back, spurred and appurtenanced like a French whore and digging her spurred boots into the flanks of the yelping fiend.

CHAPTER TWELVE

—Halligans have long memories, Angel Halligan said to himself, brooding over a camp fire, aching and paining. He drew potato sacking about his back and his mind inward, humped down into foetal form and tried to forget. But Halligans have long memories and he could not forget. He remembered the levelling they had got in the bar, the hard boot on his arse and him skittering away. Foxy had got such a wallop in the balls that they might never stir again and him the strongest of them. The family could well die out from a foul kick. He checked around his frame for injury, jarred vertebra, fine fly sprains, cranium fractures, to say nothing of tanglement and rupturing of guts. Squirming his eyes, yoga-stooped, he went inward, became his pancreas, his liver, his gall-bladder, pushed through his intestines, entered his kidneys. He was no better than he thought. It would take him a creel-load of weeks to recuperate. He would have to take his summer holidays early and go down to Galway by way of Maam Cross and take it easy by the salt water.

—Halligans have long memories, he repeated to himself.

The camp was like a military hospital, dying, half-dead, maimed; none dead, thank God, none likely to die.

Angel looked at his torn forces, felt that territory had been lost, power abdicated. Longer than Felim Halligan, his father buried in Doogary, could remember, and his mind stretched back to his great-great-grandfather, buried in Achill, the Halligans had moved like lords through the baronies, above the law. Now the man called Kelly had strode into the market-place of Belmullet and cleared father, sons, nephews out of the Spanish Ship like manure through a shed window out into a field. The Halligans felt as sodden and inert as the manure heap on a bleak February day.

It hurt his pride. The Muldoons would come to hear about it. It would be talked of in Kerry. They would speak of it in every pot house, shebeen, fair, market place and knackers yard in the country.

—How is me son, Foxy? he called to his wife.

—Something awful, as if he had been torn at by hungry bitch hounds. There is no knowing half the injuries inflicted on him. He must have been a power of a man who could maul Foxy in the way he did, a man remarkable at any gathering.

—So he was, so he was. Like a wild stallion. Will Foxy pull through?

—Most likely, but he'll be of no use to any woman. Like the jennet the seed will lodge in his belly I'm thinking.

—It's an awful thought.

—He has an ear withered and only half his teeth, she told Angel.

—It was a shocking day. I'd never thought I would live to see the like of it and the pride of us that morning setting out. We'll have to go to Galway and take the sea air until we recuperate, he said.

—We'll have to go, the whole camp of us, away from the potato blight which has struck us down, Delia told him.

The injured were scattered around the camp, outside Balla, close to a pine wood. It was a small comfortable place with little hills, containing the Halligans' confusion. A fire burned in an open space, smoke drifting up into the still air, taking its ease. There was dejected movement from dogs and thin horses nibbling unambitiously at grass. Foxy groaned dramatically under green sail cloth. Pained, concussed, bound with rough bandages, he gaped. He tried to impose some order on the events. But always the wild eye of Kelly blistered his humiliation.

—Oh mother, he called, I have a gruesome pain in me belly.

—I'd say it's your teeth. You slugged half of them.

—I'll tear that runt Kelly apart given the chance again. I

had too much drink on me. That's the reason. I carried too much drink on me. But I'll be ready the next time, he explained.

——There'll be no next time and you'll never be ready. You've taken all you'll ever take, his mother told him.

——We'll see. We'll see.

But his mind was cavorting again, as if he had been strapped to a large spinning cartwheel. His mind fell apart and he vomited. Teeth and blood spewed onto his chest.

——I knew his teeth were lodged in his guts, tormenting him, his mother said.

They spent a week in the fold of the small hills, healing spirits and injured bones. Silence fermented under the stars. A mute melancholy funeral brocade stood over the bog and among the trees. Small angers stirred in their souls. Hope sprouted a few weeks.

Figures at the flaps of tents; itchy dogs, mangey, mean, yawing about small white teeth, foraged. Man, animal, comatose, healed. Wounds scabbed. Flesh knitted. Energy sprang slowly.

Two weeks later with indiscriminate stars in conjunction, they broke camp, lifted their wounded into carts and set out for Galway, moving at night, away from the fairs, fearing friend more than foe; committed to the night like lepers on the outskirts of towns. Despair hounded their flanks, lurked behind ditches, stood behind trees. It bled their hopes, whispered in their ears, laughed in derision. It ate their minds like carrion rats, sucked their marrow like weasels. They halted at gloomy places when the thin light of morning showed beyond the trees. The day could shunt for itself. They passed old spavined horses, which could have been sold for racehorses, and left them grazing in paddocks.

There was good sun, full of thick colour. The old women knew its virtue. Wounds, welts, weals were exposed to the fiery eye of the day. It cauterised and cured buttocks, balls, lacerations of eye, ear and neck.

The Halligans recovered on the long way to Galway. Nature helped where she could. It may have been the rust in the bog streams, the tang of the heather, rabbit meat, the constant day heat on running wound and blue welt or the tough calibre of the Halligan seed which carried them back to health.

On reaching the low hills above Galway and looking down on the city and observing the sea, they felt they could hatch a plan to destroy Kelly and his two companions.

CHAPTER THIRTEEN

Kelly, Faustus, Leibide looked at the shooting lights fade.

—Me bum's wet, Leibide said when it was dark again. They had been sitting on damp heather, barnacle ague fixing itself to their backsides.

—It's an unnatural conflagration we have seen tonight, Faustus said from his pouch, a horrific experience to be such close observers to a straddled devil, a woman riding the evils of the world through a maze of lecherous lights.

—It is so, Leibide said, but you're a fair trickster with words, the likes of which I never heard used in me thirty-five years. 'Tis making them up you are as you go along.

—Indeed no. They are all in books, every one of them, ranged out in large dictionaries in alphabetical order.

—As a man needs only a cow and ten acres to get along, so also he needs only a few words to tell what's on his mind, Leibide reflected with some finish. His rhythms were borrowed from the penny catechism, something of which he was not aware.

—We'd be illiterate were it not for religion, Faustus added.

—Me bum's wet, Leibide said again, cold making him aware of the contours of his buttocks.

—We'll get some whins for kindling and a creel of turf and dry our trousers out, Kelly told them, pulling out Faustus from the inside of his shirt and dropping him to the ground. They gathered warped whins and piled them near the mouth of a hut. They piled turf about the kindling, fired it, fuelled it with more whins until sheets of flame whipped the

reluctant sods into fire. They stooped down with their backsides to the fire, silent meditators, steam rising from their
trousers.

——You did fair pounding up there, Leibide said.

——A carpentry job, Kelly told him.

——You didn't have many tools going up.

——A hammer and a nail.

——One nail?

——It was a magical nail that you would hear about in the
old stories. Once you had driven it in, secured it and rammed
it home, another nail grew again after a time.

——As fast as a mushroom? Leibide asked.

——Even faster.

Leibide browsed, looking outward into the dark, on nails.
Steam was rising from his backside, like the retreating roots
of a white rheumatic disease.

——Me bum's nice and warm now, Kelly, as if I was in bed
for a few hours.

——Good, Leibide, you'll sleep well.

——What was the nail made from Kelly, Iron? he asked.

——Bone.

——You're not serious.

——I am.

——Do you know, Kelly, I'd love a feed of bacon and
cabbage now or maybe spare ribs to chew on. Me belly is
empty, weighed down with the stones of hunger.

——It was a long day and we'll have to sleep. We'll get food
tomorrow after we have found the horse in the bog for he's
moving around in this vicinity, Kelly told them.

——He'll have to be a big horse to carry us, Leibide said.

——Indeed so. We better sleep now, Kelly said.

——I wonder where are the tinkers? Leibide asked.

——Lost in the bogs, Kelly said.

——That Foxy Halligan is a queer one. He'll have it in for
you. He's known the countryside over for the men he did
injury to.

——We'll leave our memories rest, Leibide. We'll sleep and
clean out the stables of our heads.

——Fair do's, Kelly, if you say so.

They went into the hut. Faustus lay between their two

chests of matted hair. Quickly the three fell asleep. Their snores rose and fell together and filled the dark bog and the valleys of mountains with sound. It was soft and friendly and unlike the wet damp rain.

Next morning they discovered the countryside. No soft music had ever trespassed on it. No man could build a house on its wet surface. There was no green walled patch that might be ploughed for oats, furrowed for potatoes or left fallow after crop bearing.

A jittery twitter of a lark was carried through the heather. Sinister mists, twisted, knotted, nudged each other, like a sleepy pen of sheep, above quagmire, bog-hole and bone-picked deal boles. Here and there, between swathes of bog-fog, islands of bleak sally trees.

—What's that general Cromwell said? Kelly asked.

—To Hell or to Connaught, Faustus answered.

—I'd smash the insulter's gob if I could lay me hands on him, Leibide frothed in anger, it was the likes of him that caused untold sorrow to Ireland, pitch-capped the men of ninety-eight, and tossed children onto the top of spears.

—Where did you hear that? Faustus asked.

—A master taught it to me once. His eyes were blazing red when he would talk about it. He'd beat me sometimes with a stick he had and I had to say Emmet's speech from the dock until I could say it backwards. The same teacher, the curse of Caoch Dubh on him, had me up on the ass cart the day of Jim Corley's station, saying it for half the parish. He knew all the stories about Ireland and when he'd be finished saying them, you would want to go out and die for the country.

—It's a country not worth pissing for, Faustus said, an island of neither saint nor scholar, and I know what I'm talking about.

They looked across the bog. The mist was thinning. The dreary surface of the bog appeared.

—Not a snipe, never mind a horse of any respectable bone, could survive on the whin and grass of that bog. And no man ever thought of building a house on it, Faustus commented.

—How do you know there's a horse here at all? Leibide

asked, poulticing his ear with his hand.

——A fellow told me and I can depend on him, Kelly replied.

——You're more than natural, Kelly, Leibide said.

——Maybe I am. Maybe I amn't. It's equal any way.

——Who owns the horse, Kelly? You know you could be hanged for stealing a horse in these parts, Leibide told him.

——It belonged to nobody before and it will belong to nobody again. His name is Lubach Caol.

——It's a peculiar name, Kelly, for a horse, Faustus said.

——It must be like the magical horse of Troy, Leibide said.

——What do you know about the magical horse of Troy and where is Troy?

——Troy is up the country, Leibide pointed east, and once a woman be the name of Eileen Boscus ran away from her husband with a lad called Patches, who was the handsomest man in the barony. The husband was called Manus and he gathered all the village people together. They got into their ass carts and followed them and stood outside Troy. But there was no getting in. They had built walls everywhere as Patches was popular. So for a week Manus and his men wandered about the walls and were pelted with sods of turf and rotten turnips. There was no getting in and they were getting hungry. Besides there was hay to be made into cocks at home. They were beaten until the carpenter from the village got an idea. He went behind a hill and built the ass carts into a horse and put four ass cart wheels at the bottom knees of the legs. Those who saw it said it was a great job and that you would expect the wooden horse to neigh or have a foal. It had a different type of foal. Didn't Manus and three of his men go into the belly of the horse and at night-time they brought the horse up to the walls. In the morning when Patches and Eileen saw it they thought it was a wedding present or something, so they knocked one of the stone walls and brought in the horse and looked at him.

——I knew they would give in easy enough, Patches said, seeing no one in sight, but it's a queer trophy they leave after them.

They celebrated the victory with a ceili and the fiddler came in, tuned his fiddle and started the music. While they were dancing didn't Manus and the others drop out through a trapdoor in the horse's belly. They knocked down the wall that had been built up and all the waiting men crept in. They beat the daylights out of the people of Troy, set a thatch and cock of hay on fire and they brought Eileen home. Patches got a blow of a stick on the head and always had a slate loose after that. That's the story.

—And who ever told you that story? Faustus asked.

—A blind man I met on the hills one day and me up counting sheep.

—What was his name?

—He had a queer name. I know that.

—It wasn't Homer by any chance.

—That's right, but I thought it was Hammer or something, but now that you say it like that you are probably right.

—It's beyond belief half the things I've seen and heard in this county since I strayed into that inn in Belmullet, Faustus said.

—You know about the magical horse now, Faustus? Leibide asked.

—Indeed I do, indeed I do, Faustus replied.

The story was no sooner finished when they heard a neigh from a copse of sally. It was the whinny of a jaded nag, pessimistic and untuned. They looked at the trees. Another whinney sawed the silence and left it shredded, like the clothes on a scarecrow.

Lubach Caol stuck its head around a sally bush. It was the head of a horse no man would bring to a fair. It had a long hungry face with yellow, snapping teeth, and it mashed heather thoughtfully in its mouth. The perished rubbery lips were suddy with green foam. They could see the veins on its skull from the hill.

—It couldn't be alive, and if it is, it shouldn't be, Leibide commented.

It mouched forward looking for fodder, trailing a long, bent body. It was bent in two directions, the backbone warped downwards and around so that the tail was always in view of the eye.

—We better halter it before it runs away, Kelly told them.

—It's scaffolding it needs. I wouldn't touch it, Kelly. Walk away from it and leave it seriously alone or we'll be dragging a carcass across the bog to a bone house, Leibide told Kelly. It's sickly and diseased, even from here. By normal standards it should be dead. Have no dealings with it, Kelly.

Kelly had confidence in what Tarbh had said. By the looks of it, it was only the caricature of a horse and should have fallen apart. Maybe it had fallen apart inside the leather hide, thorn-torn, scarred with dry wounds. One ear was cocked impertinently, the other flapping in the breeze, the knobby knees, the bowy legs might snap and the body collapse in a heap.

—Try and catch it, Leibide, Kelly told him.

—That's an easy matter. There is no horse born that could get away from me, and he went down the slope to the trees.

The horse's eyes followed him, as it chewed casually. When Leibide got near it the stench of its breath caught him in the throat.

—Kelly, I tell you it's diseased. Its breath stinks like a pigsty that hadn't been cleaned for twenty years.

—It couldn't be that bad, Kelly said.

—It's worse. Come down and smell for yourself, Leibide roared back.

—Catch the horse and never mind the talk, Kelly ordered.

Leibide circled to the rear. Lubach Caol's knobby front feet were lodged in a black sullen pool. It bent its head and slugged up the water. There was no leading or pulling the horse away from the water. It drank on and on. Leibide was wondering where all the water was coming from or going. Then it broke water and unleashed a twisting steam of yellow piss which sizzled like acid on the turf. On and on and on it went like a rainy day. Out it poured while he drank, and Faustus, looking down, thought that if he continued he might defile all the waters of the world. It fermented and frothed on the ground, steam rose from it and was carried across the bog, staining bog cotton and heather yellow. It must have continued for half an hour by Leibide's calculation. He did not disturb the long ritual. He had strange doubts. No horse he had ever seen, even Paddy Boughan's, watered for so long. When it had slugged the pool dry, it whinnied at the general air and continued pissing.

—Catch her by the tail and pull her out of the bog-hole, Kelly told him.

Leibide caught the scraggle of limp hair, sinking his heels in the turf for purchase. He gritted his teeth and heaved, straining his muscles to the limit. The cataract of piss continued uninterrupted, like the peaceful thought through the mind of an anchorite.

—Put spew into it, Kelly called.

—I am but I might as well be pulling at the tail of Neifin.

—Try again.

Leibide gritted his teeth, pulled. The cataract stopped.

Lubach Caol ruminated for a moment. He looked up at Leibide. Then he bucked up with his back heels, caught Leibide in the stomach and knocked him backwards into a pool of water. Leibide roared out in pain.

—He has me maimed, the bugger.

—I didn't think he had that much spirit in him, Faustus remarked, looking at the horse. They walked down to the pool and dragged Leibide on to a patch of dry heather, where he lay exhausted, his soulcase heaving.

—How are you feeling inside? Kelly asked.

—The black blight on him. It's like a dose of griped colic with forty scraping fingers where he kicked me and them tearing at the lining of my stomach.

Lubach Caol was back nibbling at the rough grass again. There was no bother or disturbance on him.

—He's aisy in his way after delivering a mortal kick like that and you would think that he hasn't the power to stir one foot in front of the other, Kelly told Leibide, who had no interest in the horse. He rolled on his back on the ground, splaying his hands over the pain.

Kelly and Faustus looked at the horse with circumspection. It was chewing away at the heather with its yellow teeth, a stench of breath coming from its nostrils.

—You better call it softly. Whistle to it like you were a lark and see if your notes carry any magical powers, Faustus told him.

Kelly whistled like a lark. The notes drifted over the bog and the sun began to shine with gold, creamy light. There was no stir from the horse.

—It's lovely music, Kelly, and such an imitation as to be real, but the horse's eye carries no cognisance of it. It is tone blind, Faustus remarked.

—There must be an answer somewhere if we could riddle it out, like the cure for ailments in the herbs, Kelly remarked.

—I'm without answers, Faustus said.

—Leave him where he is, Kelly, I'm telling you. Leave him where he is, Leibide said.

—I wonder should we try a few rowan berries on him, for something in a back partition of my mind tells me he has a peculiar love for them, Kelly told them.

A rowan tree grew on the hill, lobes of vermilion berries hanging over a stream, where patient trout waited in a pool for them to fall. Kelly had the feeling that they were magic berries, because the tree had no right reason to be growing there. It was in a suspicious magical position.

—By my knowledge of growing things but there is no accounting why that tree should be growing there and berries on it this time of year, Faustus said, counterpointing Kelly's thoughts.

—There is a lot of things that aren't arguable, Faustus, but you must give them credence. Go and gather a handful of them berries and bring them down here to me, Kelly ordered.

Faustus ran up the hill, nimble as a puck goat, and stretched out his hand for a bunch of red berries, bright as the curwhibbles in the Book of Kells. He stretched out his hand, closed them on a bunch of berries, but harvested air. He became suspicious. He snatched again but the bunch pulled away like the head of a sensitive foal. —That tree has intelligence of its own, thought Faustus, and must have a thousand eyes. He turned his back and pretended to walk way. He sprang back and held on to a swarm of berries. And quick as he did, the branch snapped up and carried Faustus with it and held him over the stream, giving him a good view of the bog.

—Kelly, he roared, hurry up here or I'll be drowned.

The voice was carried down the gentle wind to where Kelly, cross-armed, was eyeing the horse. He saw Faustus hanging above the fish pool, left the horse and ran up the hill.

——How did you get into that tangle? Kelly asked.

——I don't know. It's this queer tree. It grows up and down, this way and that according to some whim or other.

And then for some reason Faustus found himself sitting on the ground, fruit shaken from the tree, its branches in outstretched decorum above him, native and controlled, bunches of berries quiescent.

——Pick them while you can, he told Kelly.

Kelly took two bunches of berries, broke them from the branches, and put them in his pocket. Then the tree shed its leaves; its berries withered and fell into the stream. It became a bent skeleton with a charred bark. Thorns grew on it. Ivy sprouted from the ground and suckled on trunk and branches.

——That's the quickest harvest I've ever seen, said Faustus.

——It's odd, sure enough but we cannot credit our eyes, Kelly said.

They went down the hill to the black pool. Leibide lay groaning, his ribs broken, his skin marked.

——Open your mouth, Kelly ordered and he squeezed the juice of seven berries on to his tongue. He healed and jumped up. Kelly took fodder in his hand and held it to Lubach Caol's mouth. It lapped the crushed berries, with short, excited breaths, nuzzling Kelly's hand.

——We're surrounded by marvels, Leibide said, I feel now like a man who could scythe a fifteen acre meadow.

——We might as well mount the horse now and see what speed he has under his feet, Kelly told them.

——It would be a shame. His bones are no stronger than eggs shells and we would be the death of him, Leibide said.

But Kelly sprang on to the mangey back and slipped into the hollow. Leibide followed him and also slipped down into the hollow. He dragged Faustus up behind him. The three of them sat in the hollow of Lubach Caol's back. Kelly grabbed the mane, heeled the horse's belly and said giddey up. Lubach Caol whinnied at the bog, sprang across the pool and away they went.

CHAPTER FOURTEEN

With hoof-spluttering steps and frightened skitter of curlew flight, the loose-boned nag started a canter across the bog. It kicked up the sod spray, sprang over mouths of solemn pools, pacing it sprightly like steppers drawing a lady's carriage. They might have been out for a canter on the alleys of the Bois de Boulogne, it was so easy and airy.

—I can't see any of the countryside and me sitting here with my nose pressed into the cleavage of Leibide's backside, Faustus called with a weak voice into the wind.

—Hand him up here to me, Kelly said.

Leibide caught him by the collar of his coat and handed him to Kelly.

—There you are now with nothing to complain about, and Kelly put him inside his shirt and buttoned it about his neck. Lubach Caol beat out an even pace on stone, turf and soft places. They saw a clamp of turf ahead of them. It seemed that the day's excursion might end here, but swallow-like, feet thrown out like a champion, it arched over it.

—Kelly? Leibide called.

—Yes, Kelly answered.

—'Tis an amazing horse. A right racer that would carry away a gold cup at the gymkhana.

—Yes.

—It's the berries in its belly that does it. I fed a horse once on turnips and mangolds and devil a good day I ever got out of him. It must be them berries.

—It's true, Kelly said.

—And did you see the way the tree turned old in a fit

like something that had taken a bad turn? Leibide asked.

—Yes.

—I'm thinking too that it's a strange animal we have between our legs, like nothing natural that I know on a farm or in the small market squares of towns.

—'Tis you that has the keen eye, Leibide, Kelly said and left it at that.

—I'm wondering where it will all end and us tearing across the unevenness of bog like we were on a king's carpet, Leibide continued, there is no knowing what the day will bring.

They put the bog behind them running in from the lonely sea coast. Neifin was before them. It was stranded among lesser mountains, an ass's spine of white running along its back. They looked up at the inert bulk and above it the blue sky with a few thin bellies of clouds.

—He'll never make the summit, Leibide said.

—Sure we'll test him, Kelly told them.

Lubach Caol was knocking sparks from shingle and boulder, running upwards towards the highest point. He stepped so easy that he might have been at the Ballinrobe races. They stood on the summit; below them the world brown and green, the beaten silver of lakes, the distance smudged with smoky grey; westwards a muggle of hills and mountains knotted. And beyond that the eternal sea.

—It's all small and neat up so high like a plan you would put on paper, Faustus said, looking in the various directions.

—We've done a great morning's travelling, like a high wind or a mountain of a wave or the swallow from distant parts, Leibide commented.

—It's not the end yet by any measure, Kelly told them, you once expressed a wish to know where China was, Leibide, and maybe before my time has run out I'll show you. Up again and we'll feed the horse a berry or two for I've noticed that she's panting hard. We'll mount her and make away.

He took two berries from his pocket and fed them to the horse. It lapped them into its mouth and chewed them for a long time as if they were fat fields of meadow grass. It licked the juice from its lips and neighed with satisfaction. It winked at Leibide.

—I'd swear that that horse knows what's going on in my mind.

—Up you go and we'll be on our way, Kelly told them.

They took their positions on the horse and turned her towards Clew Bay, Croagh Patrick and the snarl of long Galway mountains beyond that. The clouds had come up with bellies of rain. Bonhams of showers suckled a rainbow.

—Hup and at it, Kelly ordered.

Lubach Caol stiffened its crooked back, ran across the brow of the mountain and leaped towards the rainbow.

—We'll be smothered to death on the rocks or drowned in the sea, Leibide complained, lamenting a fall from the sky, horrified by the presumptive horse. But up Lubach Caol went like a ship under full canvas and some strange wind carried him with awkward grace and firmness.

—Look at the lovely islands below us, like a nest of hens eggs, Leibide said with delight.

Below them on the seaweed of the bay three hundred islands were scattered, unhatched by the cold beating tides. They moved in a slow arc above the troubled winds of the world, their eyes looking down over the side of the horse. The mortals among them were seized by fright, usurping the paths of the wheeling birds shouldering out the view which the gods have of the world.

—The affairs of men are of small proportion, not deserving much attention, Faustus said from Kelly's tranquil shirt, and one could waste acres of his time sowing their insignificant seed. From up here chapel and birthing bed, battle-field, tavern and graveyard are as trivial as children's toys.

The eyes of Faustus were looking again and the cleavage of his brain knitting into sanity.

—Fairly spoken, Faustus, Kelly said, it's a fair world in a general way but in another of great insignificance for men that see it like myself and yourself, and the great raimeis that goes on and the blood that is spilt over small fields and boundary ditches and the circumspection you find in small towns.

Leibide, never certain of his balance even on an ass and

him travelling between slow road walls, leaned over and fell
from the horse. Like Icarus, he should have plummeted into
the sea. Instead he found himself glued to the sides of
Lubach Caol. He looked up at the bald belly of the horse. His
complaints were halted by a shot of horse piss in the mouth
and he was silent until they landed on the top of Croagh
Patrick. As soon as they touched the ground, Leibide fell
from his position like a dropped foal. The wind had dried his
wet shirt and left it sparkling with the dust of diamonds.

——Be all that's high and holy, the King of Spain would
pay a ransom to have me shirt on his back, he said, brushing
away the dust, I've seen more today than was ever written
down in any of MacGinty's books.

They took their ease above the sea, lying between the
boulders like whores on luxurious beds.

——You can't eat scenery, Kelly, Leibide said, and though
I'm no man to complain, it looks like a week since the taste
of meat was on me tongue, or the juice of a drink on me lips.
It was a thin night last night and we have very little to eat.

A maw of hunger was crawling around in his stomach,
scraping its claws against its lining. It often came out of its
niche and moved about when his meals did not come
regularly.

——Wait awhile now and we'll call into an eating house or
some such place to equip ourselves. Can you wait?

——If you have a dead corpse on your hands, it won't be
for the want of a warning, Leibide told Kelly.

It was a quiet day now with a crisp wind dying to a small
breath. They lay for an hour between the protection of the
small boulders looking out at the sea. Leibide grumbled for
food, wishing that it were spread in front of him on linen
with the faded celtic patterns and the pictures of castles and
round towers that he had seen out on Jim Corley's table for
the station. But the others, with wisps of reflective heather
between their teeth, siphoned the beauty of the day into
their eyes and filled their lungs with air.

——Grace O'Malley lived on yonder island in the mouth of
the bay and kept her fleet tethered to her bed. She was a
woman ever on the alert, Kelly told Faustus.

——The beautiful Grace O'Malley, Faustus reflected, taking

the coarse grass stem from between his teeth.

——Is it mad you are? She was no beauty but a large horse of a woman, six feet two in her stockings and like a barrel of lard and no teeth in her head, Kelly told him.

——And the lovely stories they tell, Faustus said.

——She wasn't like that at all. Hard as granite and used every man she married to gain possession of the world under us.

——'Tis strange, 'tis passing strange, Faustus said.

——If she was that size she must have had a great appetite, Leibide complained weakly.

——I think we'd better go in search of food, Kelly said and he gave a whistle for Lubach Caol. They mounted his back and were off.

A jump from the mountain to a foot hill and another jump brought them to the town of Louisburgh. They ambled down the three armed town to the market place, the horse moving with sagging steps. The three riding his back, knowing his keen intelligence by now, felt that there was something in his head. They gave him his pace through the town. His hollow hoof beats filled the streets, bringing drinkers out from gloomy pubs, women from their talk and washing, at the curiosity of the noise.

——Stand by him both of you and I'll go in search of meat and drink, Kelly said to Leibide and Faustus.

They stood in the square on either side of the horse's head. The crowd came over to see the wonder. In all their lives they had never seen such a spectacle ever in the travelling circus. They circled around viewing the wonder from all considerable angles. They looked at his teeth and belly. They did not talk. Words came slow like potato tubers.

——You are strangers here, a big ponderous man said finally.

He had a squint in his eye and spoke in no unfavourable way.

——'Tis true, Leibide said.

——Are ye from Mayo?

——Parts of it, Leibide said.

——What parts?

——Up north, beyond the mountains on the far side of the

bay, Leibide continued.

——Did you come by Westport?

——No, Leibide said, the horse here is a great jumper and we came over the islands and landed on Croagh Patrick.

There was a guffaw of laughter from the frame of on-lookers. ——That horse wouldn't make bone meal, never mind jump. It's amazed I am that he didn't fall dead under the weight of you. Carrying him between you, you should be, an old woman said from out her shawl.

——He'd race any horse in Louisburgh, let me tell you, Leibide said.

They laughed again and grinned at each other, nodding and winking and pointing to their heads.

——He'd race any horse in Louisburgh, Kelly's voice said from outside the crowd, if you'd care to take on wagers and find a big field.

——The townland will give you thirty to one against your old mare if you are willing to race him up in Ned Joyce's field, the voice of the crowd said.

——Go and gather your earnings and we'll place the bets, Kelly directed.

It was easy money to every eye. So off they went back to their houses. There wasn't a penny in stockings or mattresses which was not carried back. Kelly stood with a sack and they poured the money in, the parish priest standing with a ledger and writing the sums down as they were thrown into the sack.

——Let's see the colour of your own money or there may be no wager at all, they said.

Kelly took out gold from his trousers pocket and handed it to the priest. He looked at it and passed it as real. They walked out to the edge of the town to Ned Joyce's field. News was sent to Ger Guilfoyle to saddle his racer, put on his colours and come down to the field. They marked out the course. It was a mile round and it would be a six miles race. It was like a circus ground with excitement, flags fluttering, colours flying, people running here and there, splattering whitewash on the course.

——A fool and his money are soon parted, somebody said looking at the three strangers, dragging and pushing the horse.

Lubach Caol was stuck to the square when they went to move him. Kelly and Leibide put a shoulder each to his rump and Faustus pulled. No noticeable move. The people of the town came down to the square. One half pulled and the other half pushed. If they couldn't get the horse to the starting line there could be no wager. They sweated and heaved until they got him out to Ned Joyce's field, and dragged him to the starting post. Ger Guilfoyle was there in his jockey cap and shirt, his racer saddled in new leather.

—Is he alive or dead? . . . he called.

—Alive enough to begin the race, somebody told him.

—Well, put us under starter's orders and we'll get down to it, Ger Guilfoyle said.

Lubach Caol lay on the ground, the bronze replica of himself.

—Who'll ride her, Kelly? Leibide asked.

—No better man than yourself, Kelly told him.

—I was never in a race in me life, Kelly.

—Never mind. Get up on his back and wait for the signal from the parish priest.

Leibide did as he was ordered. He sat on Lubach Caol uncertainly. He was breathing hard, coughing with coarse asthma.

—Ready, your reverence, they told the parish priest.

The parish priest waved his handkerchief and the race started. Away galloped Ger Guilfoyle, the fortunes of the town on his back. Lubach Caol remained where he stood and refused to budge. They kicked at him, prodded his hide, twisted his tail, jumped in front of him. He was unconcerned. It would be no race at all. Guilfoyle's horse kicked up sods with great alacrity. Round he went five times, gallant and serious. He was on his last lap when Lubach Caol gave a start. He shuddered and staggered down the course. —He's moving! Hurray, they roared.

But then he let a large fart as if all the winds of the world had come untwisted inside him and started running. Some said that he did not run at all but flew. Lubach Caol stretched out so long that his belly touched the ground and his feet kicked up the wet scraw. Around he flew like a constricted electron or a hawk swooping through a cloud of sparrows or a whale through a school of herring. The air opened in front of him and closed behind. Ger Guilfoyle was almost swept off his horse by the eddying winds. Leibide, cross-eyed with fear, feet around the horse's neck, his face buried in the flying seaweed mane, thought that the bravest heart would soften to jelly and slobber at the turn of events. A frame of sighs and lamentations rose from the crowd, sown on the margin of whitewash. The mysterious horse was running away with every penny they had collected into bags and stockings, stuffed into mattresses or pushed down into the metal tubes of four-poster beds. Days as bleak as winter lay ahead of them if Ger Guilfoyle's horse could not stir his legs faster. It was a communal madness to bet in the first place, like a general disease in cattle or on stalks.

Five times Lubach Caol coursed around, going so fast that Ger Guilfoyle's horse might not be moving at all. However fast he was, they thought that he was much slower. A sacristy bell sounded the last lap as Lubach Caol tore across the starting line and down the course like the hammers of hell. No stopping him now, only the finishing post to be passed. He was ten feet of being home and dry when he stopped and fell on the ground. Leibide continued in full flight, first home. He concused his brain against the wall of his skull. Constellations of flying stars brought a pleased grin to his subconscious face.

Faustus like a dervish danced about the recumbent horse, which started to eat the grass of the field leisurely.

——It's no time for eating daisies, he cried at him, let us down now and we'll be the laughing stock of Mayo.

——You might as well leave him there and bury him because no known horse could stand that pace, an onlooker said.

——Clear the way, clear the way. Ger is in the final straight. Leave way for the victor, the jubilant crowd ordered.

And so it seemed.

Kelly dragged Leibide by the heels to the horse and threw him backside up on its back.

He kicked the rump of Lubach Caol.

——Come on you stiff-boned hippogriff and daffodil eater,

are you going to let me down in me worst hour of want?

—Spectators off the course, the parish priest called.

Kelly stood in front of Lubach Caol and eyed him. Their minds locked like fingers. Kelly saw Ger Guilfoyle, jacket fluttering, bearing down on him. Quick as a wink, he popped five berries into Lubach Caol's mouth.

—I should kick the hocks off you, you blackmailer, he roared at him.

Ger Guilfoyle was past them and seemed a winner, but Lubach Caol with a great spring sailed over his head, like a salmon taking a weir, and landed beyond the post. It was a jump worth a lot of money.

—He's a winner, they groaned, and by the anvils of Cromwell's blacksmiths we have lost our last halfpenny.

—It wasn't a race at all but a flying match. Sure no horse is capable of such supernatural powers since the Fermorians brought the first horse to Ireland. He wiped all our eyes by the seclusion of his speed and agility, they complained.

—It isn't a foal you'd knock out of that one but a hawk, was remarked by somebody.

The parish priest, with a good knowledge of the turf and the powers of evil loose in the world, knew that the horse had something more than a strange pedigree. He took up his sacristy bell and started across the fields home.

—Carry over the sack of money here to me now, for it has been fairly won by a good horse, Kelly ordered.

—That isn't a horse at all, but only something resembling a horse and should have a different name, an old woman complained.

—No twisting words as if you were before the justice. It was a horse when we started the race and you all eager to rob us of any penny we had. It was a fair race and nobody ever knew all the particulars of a horse at the starting line. It's in the unevenness the chance lies, Kelly told them.

Leibide lay in the valley of the horse's back, inert as a sack of meal, his mind still swarming with a hive of stars. And all his life in a splintered mirror of images, the colour of can-sweets, appeared before him.

Kelly lifted Faustus into position and leaped up beside Leibide. Placing the sack of money on Leibide's back he heeled the flank of the horse and started him back towards the small town to the barrel of porter and a side of bacon in the market square.

The head-bowed funeral train trailed sorrowful feet after them, muttering wake-house solemnities to one another. They might have been following their dead home from battle or accompanying a relative to an American emigrant ship.

—It went fast when it went and me thinking it would last for years, one woman said with bent head.

—There is no telling the way chance throws the dice, or what black bad luck the wind carries. Who would think and the sun rising beyond the mountains this morning that disaster would come riding down the road in from Westport on a spavined nag? her husband asked.

—It's like a wake without drink, pipe or tobacco, a voice muttered. —Outside disbelieving anything but the Creed, I have my doubts about what we have seen today, another voice said. —It's peculiar that such a weak-boned horse should carry such power within him and a heavy proportioned man on his back.

In one sense no single voice said any of these words. They were the voice of a sad townland lamenting a disaster as bad as the famine. A gloom settled on the town when they reached the square as it does at an open grave. But Kelly had great good humour. He knew that no one is ever happy unless he is sad, that you cannot banish a cloud on a sunny day and that barren women wish for a harvest. He stopped Lubach Caol at the barrel and side of bacon and stood on the barrel.

Below him, heads considered the cobblestones of the square. Kelly rattled the bag of money for attention. They looked up at him.

—I suppose if I had the parish priest's reckoning book here and was quick cyphering, I could tell you whether it is eight hundred or a thousand pounds I have here in the bag.

—It must be close on a thousand, a voice said.

—Without money you can neither buy or sell. Money is not a thing easily come by, and a wise man and his money are soon parted when he thinks he is transacting with a fool, Kelly told them.

——We'll remember that, sir, till our dying day.

——I have no intention of carrying this money away from here. It is far too heavy. But I'm a man sent from England by the Queen to make the people of Ireland value their money.

——God bless the Queen, they chanted.

——And this is a government horse fed on special oats from Arabia, sown when the moon is in eclipse, he continued.

——It's you in the big city have all the knowledge, they commented.

——And now I'll give you the money back on condition that the hospitality of the town will always be open to my two friends when they come walking the road.

——Consider it done, sir.

——And what's more, the money which has been in a magical bag of mine has been growing away here and every man will get one and a half times his share when I ladle it out to you.

Kelly, Faustus and Leibide might have been rain gods, they were so popular when the news of the good fortune spread. The parish priest, having heard of the turn of events, rushed into the market place brandishing his note book. By the time the money was distributed the moon had matured into a brown edible cheese in the pantry of the skies. A turf fire, three times the height of a man, was lit and tables drawn into the market square. A blind fiddler, coming home from Galway and trying to reach his people and stand among them somewhere in east Mayo, was put sitting on a chair beside the fire. He tightened the strings of his fiddle, nibbled at them with his fingers to get tone. He nodded his head in satisfaction and, finally, drew his bow across the strings and the dancing started. Next morning many a girl and mature woman found hay in her skirts. For Kelly's eye was glowing white. He was setting his crop. ——It was a wild night, they often said afterwards, when they looked at the redheaded lads running around the weighing scales in the square. They said that Kelly was a reprobate and that the devilment he worked in Louisburgh he had worked in all the small towns. They said that Kelly and horse were in collusion, tricking honest people into harmful ways. They said also that he was a liar, that oats didn't grow in Arabia, and that the Queen, who was a chaste woman, would have nothing to do with him.

But next morning when the three left it was to the sound of Goodbyes and You're always welcome in Louisburgh. In the young girls' eyes and the eyes of women who should have more sense, a wise man could read the stirrings of a rich harvest.

CHAPTER FIFTEEN

The Halligans trailed into Galway, wasted, woebegone after thirteen nights' journeying, keeping constantly to unmetalled roads. During the days, leper-hidden, they suppurated in quarry, wood or deserted village, as shy as deer. A bleak melancholy lay on their souls, like green scum on water. It poisoned their movements, corroded the ring of their talk, shuffled their feet. There were some brave words now and then in the tidy locality of a night fire, when they imagined themselves at prime fettle, hooped in strength, booting the fundaments of Kelly with hobnailed boots, heeling him with tipped heels into the ribs and sieving his head with a rain of blows from a blackthorn stick. By the time they reached Galway the instruments of torture had been itemized in their minds; reaping hooks to slit his throat, a bayonet to twist the twine of his guts, a ninety-eight pike to prize out the jewel of his eye, a pig emasculator, silver-sharp as a surgical instrument, a bag of salt to smarten wounds. Their imaginations had never been more active as they pictured the brutalities to themselves. They tempered their despair with the determination to have unholy revenge.

Angel Halligan had gone into the decline ever since the day they had broken camp in Balla. He groaned in the open cart, the bump of every stone running through his body. He wished he were in the clay, buried with those who had died during summer migrations to Galway.

—Take it as easy as you can, Angel, Foxy said, in five more nights we'll be in the city of Galway and we'll get the best healers in town to cure you.

——Ah, Foxy lad, there is no curing. I'm bunched. I'm at the very end of my days. I'll never live to see another summer and I'll never spit on the palm of my hand again and close a bargain.

——That's no talk from a man with a heart like you. Sure no Halligan ever said good-day to life at an early age.

——There was Red Tom, Angel replied.

——He fell from a Protestant steeple stealing lead. Natural disaster cannot be counted.

——Well, Kelly is a natural disaster, Foxy.

——They'll be scraping him off ditches when I get me hands to him, for we'll flail the daylights out of him and the chaff of his bones will be blown down every twisty road in the baronies.

——'Tis no use talking, Foxy. I'll never come to next January. We are caught in the tangle of things and the spotted spider of death is always spinning his fine thread, Angel said in a brooding voice.

——Stop your gob, father. By every nanny goat's udder and the beauty of Kate Houlihan, a wash in the seaweed baths will leave you better than you ever were before.

——No, son. There is an awful blackness festering inside me like a dark shower over a lake. It was your man in Belmullet that is the cause of my ailment. That mad eye of his turning in his head has withered the juices of my soul.

——By the Babylonian captivity and every acre of sea-grass in the country, I'll rip open his gullet and drain his blood into a bog hole and bury him under scraws.

——Easy with airy words, son.

——There'll be others too, eager to square accounts with him.

——He has the power, son. He has the power son.

They held many conversations on their way to Galway, Angel passing on to his son any wisdom he might have picked up during the years. In exile in Galway, close to the sea, with the priest present, ballast in his soul to stabilise it on the seas of eternity, Angel Halligan died. No natural causes could be given for his death, except that his spirit had been broken by the misfortunes of Belmullet. Tribes and sub-tribes came to the wake when word went out. They laid him out, hands joined, peace on his face, in a coffin of oak with silver mountings, in a house they had hired. Four tall candles standing to the north, east, west and south corners of the coffin warded off evil. They threw a pious light on the face of Angel in the quiet pool of death.

——You did him well in the end, Delia, a woman sympathiser said to Delia Cuff sitting in the corner, there is no King at Buckingham Palace was ever sent off in such style.

——He was decent and true to the bit of light given him, Delia said.

——He was that and no better man knew how to judge a horse, or mend a milking bucket, the sympathiser continued.

——Well it's all over for him, and there is no bringing him back, Delia Cuff said with finality.

At the beginning there was a frame of reverence about the body; men coming through the door with hats and caps crumpled against their breasts, ready with doleful, wake comments. ——Musha, he looks calm and even, without a distress on his mind. And there is many an archbishop and lawyer that lay in his coffin with a troubled look on his face.

——It's a fair ending to a hard life. He reared a fine family and paid all his bills. He never stole a thing but it wasn't needed by those for whom he took it.

When they sat, eye level with the coffin, they were given a coil of tobacco like tow rope to cut from. Then they were given a clay pipe. When they were puffing, they had a glass of whiskey put into their hands.

——God spare the living and may he show mercy to the dead, but they were few like Angel Halligan.

Halligan seemed to grin as his white, waxy ears listened to the fine speeches of praise fluttering about him like crows wings.

The parlour room, kept for the priest below the kitchen and used on the rare occasion when there was a death or a station, was ringing with loud talk, as the early arrivals continued to wake the corpse. The memories started by the stiff, rigorous corpse, reverent under the religious glow of candles, had startled the pack of hounds of their memories from barking kennels. No man is alone. He is one of a tribe and he is only a branch of a tree. Porter ran from wooden barrels stacked on the sideboard, and every mugful carried some exaggerated memory or other. There was augmentation and correction. —Do you remember the night we took on the Peelers below in Ballina after coming from the fair of Cross-molina? The streets ran red with blood that night. Martin Wade was born next morning in the prison cell, Tossy Halligan recalled.

—That's right, it was like a battlefield. The magistrate said that the likes of the Halligans never wore shoe leather, Casta continued.

—There was never the likes of us, and there is no man living but is afraid to meet us and outanger us.

They were silent when they thought of Kelly but broke out talking again and forgot, for the warm porter told them that the whole sorry business had been a mistake and that some dark night in the future they would throttle him, fair and square.

Down in the corpse room the keening women started an Egyptian cry that had thin bones and yellow skin. It would wake the dead if there was any spark among the ashes. They tore their grey hairs with chapped fingers, combing away the lice of sorrow, twisting their bodies this way and that in desolation. Angel Halligan with great patience and absence of mind lay still in the coffin. If there was a good mare in heaven, he was on his way to finding it. He had a good eye for a beast, but sapphires, diamonds or jade were beyond him.

On the fire, dirty bubbles shouldered up under the skillet pot lid and told the women that the potatoes had burst their coats and bared their chests. The pigs' crubeens were stewing nicely too, plopping soupy bubbles. The smell released a feeling of hunger in the gathered stomachs. The women caught the crook of the skillet pot with a potato sack and took it off the fire. They drained the scummy water and heeled the potatoes onto the table where they steamed dry. The men came and took them, peeled them and rolled them cold in the palms of their hands.

It was hard to know who started the potato battle. It might have been Humpy Sheamus with a bitter twisted humour. Whoever it was, Paud Halligan got a warm potato in the ear which scalded him. He roared in pain and dropped the crubeen from his hand. He saw the malicious grin on Humpy Sheamus's eye and, gathering a fist of potatoes, hurled them at him. Soon potatoes hailed in all directions, hitting friend and enemy. The battle started. It was carried on around the tranquil island of the coffin. Potatoes stuck to the wall, were pulped into the ground. Fragments fell into the coffin, and in the din the coffin was turned over and out fell Angel Halligan on the floor, his hands joined in reverence. When the cone of potatoes in the middle of the table was exhausted the battle stopped as quickly as it began. They lifted Angel back into the coffin, righted the candles and munched repentant thoughts from the salty crubeens. The men returned to the parlour again and tapped another barrel of porter.

On the third evening the body of Angel Halligan was ripe for burial. With the wake activities they almost forgot that there was a burial at hand.

——Call in the musicians and we'll have a dance, Foxy ordered.

They cleared the room of Christian symbols and the coffin was slanted against the end wall. The rigor of death held Angel in a stiff sentry position.

To the drinking was now added the airy activity of dancing. The bard of the family, John Sebastian Halligan, unslung his accordion from his back and started into the music. He was a bit of a wonder among them, the only musician in a long line of dour men. He went from market place to market place playing the accordion and selling ballad sheets with chapbook illustrations on them.

Up and down the floor they went, hopping and shouting, advancing and retreating to the waves of the music. Sweat steamed from the faces of the men and from under the petticoats of the women with the great heat in the small area.

The serious men played cards. Women nursed babies to sleep. Some stayed close to the barrels of stout. People continued to come into the house.

——Tell me this and tell me no lie, a stranger said, but are we at a wedding or a wake?

——Well I couldn't tell you rightly. The door was open and

I came in.

—Ask somebody.

—Is it a wedding or a wake? they asked one of the Halligans.

—A wake.

—Well may the lord have mercy on the dead. Man or woman?

—Angel Halligan.

—Well may he rest in peace and resurrect glorious.

—Is he buried?

—No, but the cart should be ready at any hour. There he is standing over there in the coffin pious looking.

—A grander corpse never closed an eye. He looks so well standing there that you would think he might hop out and join in the dancing.

—'Twas his own wish to be placed there I believe. He said that if he didn't come out and join them after three days he was surely dead for he couldn't resist the sound of a reel.

—And who are you? . . . the tinker Halligan asked the women who had been asking him all the questions.

—The wife of the rag and bone man.

—And where is he?

—He went in before me.

—You don't want a man to go out after you?

—Well, I wouldn't say no.

She went out to the backstreet where the husband had tethered the ass with the rag cart. They found the rags soft and comfortable.

Foxy Halligan knew the value of money. Why cover extra distance by going to the church past the cemetery and coming back again? Or why have gravediggers in your employ and the strongest men in Connaught drinking your porter?

—Come up here to me, he said to the strongest men he could find, go out and get five shovels and go down and dig a grave. We'll give you a lead of an hour and then we'll be after you with Angel in the cart.

They went.

Three hours later they shouldered the coffin onto the street and put it on the back of a decorated cart. Foxy took the halter, sat up on the coffin and led the cortege. He was so scattered drunk that he circulated the graveyard twice before he found the gate. The five idiots sent to dig the grave had got bored waiting and had dug an extra grave.

—What put it into your heads to dig two graves? Foxy asked.

—We thought that he was such a decent man that he should have a choice. It would give you a chance to pick a nice cushiony resting place for him.

—It sounds reasonable, Foxy said, let me look into them.

He bent over the lip of the first grave and looked into its whale's belly. He overreached himself and fell in. His moans came up hollow.

—Are you dead, Foxy? somebody called down.

—Cripes I'm not. Keep them five idiots away from the heap of clay or they will start throwing it in on top of me.

They got a ladder and Foxy came up from the grave.

—What was it like down there Foxy? they asked.

—Something awful, he told them, a dark passageway into hell.

They lowered the coffin of Angel Halligan into the grave and shovelled the clay down on him.

—Say a few words, Foxy, somebody prompted.

—Jim Lonergan's bar is open and if you traipse down there now, I'll buy you all a drink, Foxy said.

—Say something about your father, they prompted.

—Me father would have done the inviting himself but I'm afraid he's beyond the want of drink now.

Jim Lonergan was in no humour to serve the Halligans drink as they poured into the door like a pig mash into a trough.

—Drinks for everybody, Jim, Foxy called with familiarity.

—There will be no drinks for none of your class. Your father was a decent man and if he were here I'd serve you, but seeing he isn't you can go and whistle for them.

—If he were here, you would serve us? Foxy asked.

—Indeed I would, for no decenter man ever stood on a stool, not like the likes of them that came after him, Lonergan told him.

Foxy Halligan looked around.

—Now you all sit still for a moment and me and me

brothers will be back in the next to no time.

He went out the door with his brothers and left the rest sitting round on benches like sheep in a pen outside a slaughterhouse. They looked at one another and down at the floor. Jim Lonergan cleaned the glasses with ritual. A half an hour later they burst through the door. Angel Halligan had his arms around their shoulders.

—Well will you look who we found walking through the graveyard and him pretending to be dead? As you said, Jim, he's the finest man that ever sat at the counter and ordered a pint. So pints all round and don't delay for we are all of us thirsty.

—You're beaten, Lonergan, they called, serve out the porter as you said you would.

Afraid of the evil trickling through the universe, he pulled the pints of stout. Then he escaped out the back. Again there was dancing to the music of John Sebastian Halligan.

For a week they held out in Lonergan's pub. Finally the Peelers erected a battering ram on the blind side of the house. The music had ceased and there was a strange quiet within. When they breached the wall and went inside, the Halligans lay on the floor, like a town visited by a pestilence. They recognised the corpse from the joined hands and the shroud. They took Angel Halligan and returned him to the cemetery where he was buried in peace. The rest of the tribe was carried down the street and put in prison to await the pleasure of a magistrate.

It was summer time and there was great extension in the days.

CHAPTER SIXTEEN

They left Louisburgh with great ceremony and decorum. The crowd trailed after them, waving and dancing, until they reached the bridge. Kelly, Faustus and Leibide rode down the main street like champions, a keg of porter and a side of bacon strapped across the withers of Lubach Caol. They turned right and headed for Roonah Quay. It was a morning of golden wonder and firm sequence, not a breath among the sand grasses, the even advent and whip of waves and their fallow, metrical retreat pleased their eyes. The sky was threaded with the wheeling flight of sea gulls, their cries stippling the silence.

Lubach Caol padded across the sands with neat hoof steps down to Tonakeera Point. A leap over Killary harbour landed them at Cleggan, within sight of the towering shoulders of the Twelve Pins. They headed for Galway, following a circuitous path. Leibide was full of wonder at the wideness and the length of the world, as if it had no limits and no end. Clearly there were more people in it than he had ever seen congregating at Tobar Church or driving cattle into Eaglais. But always the landscape was of peat and brown water, small lakes with bull rushes and moor hens and singular white swans.

——I've a remark to make, Kelly, Leibide said.

——Make it, Leibide, Kelly encouraged.

——I am going to draw your attention to something which might have slipped your notice. Ireland for the most part is surrounded by water and Ireland surrounds much water by way of a lake.

——We'll have to wait and see for ourselves, Kelly told him.

——And another thing, he continued, if you keep going around the coast of Ireland you'll come back to where you started from.

——It's you that has the observant eye, Kelly told him.

Away to the east, beyond the backs of the mountains, Kelly knew that Kate Houlihan, intact, tower-housed, looked down on the waters of Lough Corrib. He had heard much talk of her intelligence and her beauty. His spirit ached for this woman and he felt singular and sad like the swan he had seen in a lake. The wildness within him was broken. A part of him wished for quieter days, the even fill and fall of the tide.

He banished the feelings from his mind.

They reached Galway, with its gates and twelve tribes and the memory of wine ships and Spanish gold. It was noon now, a time of slow activity, the spread of sails seeking to catch the shy presence of wind; harbour calls, small boats plying the water, silver mackerel scattered on the granite slabs of the pier; nets stretched to dry, the tang of salt and seaweed. They followed narrow streets to a small tavern where, in the cool shadows and on deal tables, they drank wine. They fell into reminiscence.

——In the days when I collected tombstone inscriptions I once heard of a great poteen maker in Kerry, but he lived up in the mountains between the Paps and I never had time to visit him.

——What type of man was he? Kelly asked.

——Full of knowledge they said. A man who took great pride in his work.

——We should visit that man, Leibide Ludden said.

——And so we will, Kelly told them, anxious for activity, for the luxury of wine and the coolness of the tavern had reminded him of Kate Houlihan and he wished to be away.

And so they mounted Lubach Caol and with magical speed they were in Kerry. Faustus MacGinty had a great affection for the people of Kerry. It might have been the mountains with their hidden places, their talk like delicate scroll work, which twisted and turned and tangled like the ornaments on

old books and crosses. It might have been the Paps carrying
erect nipples of stone, as if the county were a sensual woman,
her back on the ground, her generous thighs open to the sea.

—Look for the Paps and you will find the poteen maker's
house in the dip between them.

Night was now coming on, the stars firm in the darkness.

They found the Paps and between the Paps they
discovered the house. The door was open and Kelly entered.
The old poteen maker, lying in his caileach, was dying. A
small candle-butt guttered in a pool of wax and it could have
been his spirit trying to wade out of his old flesh. He was
fragile and bright eyed with a small nibbly head like a robin.

—Oh it's not a small devil from hell come to bear away
my soul, while the big ones are out carrying away the souls
of the rich, he said to Faustus when he entered the kitchen.

—No, Faustus said.

He was reassured by the monosyllable.

—Then you are not the law boys down from the Castle
looking for a still?

—No. We're not. My name is Kelly, Kelly said directly.

—Not the Kelly the delph seller was talking about last
week when he called at the door? He said there is a new
proverb in the language which states And when they heard
the name of Kelly, they all flew like midges.

—The very same, Kelly told him.

—Well you are welcome and you will surely put a bit of
heart into me, knowing that in a hundred years time people
will be talking about you. By the beauty of Kate Houlihan,
but you are welcome. What brought you up the crooked
road to my house?

—I'll tell you straight, poteen maker, but we heard of
your great skill and, knowing that there is not a drop of your
drink left in Ireland, we said we would come and visit you.

—Ah Kelly, my hero, but the last barrel of poteen I made
was ten years ago, for a cousin of mine up in a monastery in
the midlands. He minds cattle. Sure he plagued me for the
secret but I couldn't let it get into the wrong hands, for it is
a drink intended for kings or men bent on poetry. And it is
hard to get the ingredients.

His voice was faulty and slow and came through phlegm

lodged in his throat.

——And tied to this bed I can't see if the moon and the stars are right and holding the condition of things in nice proportions.

——Well Faustus MacGinty here has a great knowledge of the stars and he can go to the door and call out their position for you relative to the Paps.

——Fair do's to him, but I didn't think the little man would have such extensive knowledge in his head and me taking him for a small urchin or a devil.

——He's one of the great geniuses in Ireland, that little fellow, and you could fill a library with all that's in his head. Kelly told him.

——You are telling me no lie?

——Upon my solemn oath, poteen maker.

——Well let him go outside the door and call out the condition of the moon and the position of the stars.

Faustus stood at the door, looked up between the Paps at the wheeling heavens and called out the number and the position of the stars relative to the moon.

——The tides in the heavens are full. It is time to make the great drink but there are things wanting from the four corners of Ireland.

——Fetching them is no great problem, for I have a horse grazing outside that goes as quick as greased lightning.

——You have, have you?

——Upon my oath, poteen maker.

——Well take pencil and paper, the poteen maker directed. Kelly did.

——Inscribe as follows. Whins from the plains of Kildare. Summer barley which has been fermented for three weeks as near as possible to the rock of Cashel. A tubing fifteen feet long of Wicklow copper and an iron barrel well scoured from the port of Waterford. You get them requirements and we're well on the way to making good poteen.

It was a night of activity among the mountains as if Hercules himself were at labour. They groaned and sweated. They stole turf and started a fire and put Kildare whins into the barrel that the wash might catch the scent of aromatic flowers.

For the moment the poteen maker had given up any notion he ever had of dying. There was great glee in his eyes as he directed the alchemists. He winked when he heard the bubbles burst thickly in the barrel. Leibide carried bucket after bucket of water from the well to cool the coiling worm. Faustus MacGinty and Kelly sat on the bed beside the poteen maker and watched the rite with great solemnity.

The poteen maker began to reminisce, while the poteen dripped into a bucket. He had dug potatoes in Scotland, he had unloaded ships in California, he had panned for gold in South America, he had been on the roads to Paris, Rome and Lisbon, he had spent a summer lumbering in Russia, which was within sight of China, and he had slept nights on the spice islands.

——The more you see, the more you wonder, and the more you know, the less you know, he wheezed.

——Tell me now, poteen maker, did you ever hear of Kate Houlihan?

——All men have heard of Kate Houlihan. But no one has ever seen her close except the old women and the senile masters.

——Why the mystery about this woman? Is she not a normal man's daughter?

——Not now. Mad Houlihan brought her to the castle on the Corrib as a child to educate her. They say she is the fairest woman in Ireland and knows all that is to be known. Mad Houlihan will only mate her with the best blood in Europe. She's a lonely woman who stands at her tower window and looks at the stars. She is fit only for the best of men. Have you seen her Kelly?

——No, but I have heard the talk of her beauty.

——A soul companion to a man, Kelly. You have dreams about this woman?

——I have.

——Well perhaps she too has had her dreams about you Kelly, for your story has spread far.

Kelly walked to the door and looked up at the shining heavens and the sad gaps between the stars and thought about Kate Houlihan.

There was much talk in the small thatched house during

the next few weeks. Then they put the poteen through the worm for the final run. They filled six barrels in all. It was the last run of poteen the poteen maker would ever supervise.

——Bring me a mug of poteen. Bring us all a mug and may it keep sergeant death away from the door for a while more.

They drank a mug of poteen each, except Faustus, who sipped only a little. They felt solemn on the sad occasion for they knew that the last of the great distillers was dying. But the warm liquid in his mouth brought a little life back into him. He sat up in bed with an eagerness of eye.

——Now that I have high fire in me, Kelly, I will sing a song for you from your own part of the country called *Stacking Gold,* but before I do I want you to promise me that you will play a trick on a cousin of mine down in Cork. He is a parish priest and a serious man, not like the cousin who minds cattle up in the midlands. He is parish priest of Cosruthan.

——I will do that, Kelly promised.

——Well with that promise given, I'll sing.

He lifted his mug and began.

There are many ways of collecting pieces,
And heaping treasures in stacks of gold.

But before the ending the voice gave a splutter and the coughing of death seized him. He spewed out the last mouthful of drink on the bedclothes. The fall of the dice was against him and he said nothing before he died but what he sung.

They dug a grave for him between the Paps. He was the last of a long race of distillers and the likes of him would not be seen again on the stretches of human sand cast up by the unaccountable sea.

They strapped the remaining barrels to the side of Lubach Caol like ceremonial drums and mounted the horse. With a sad tuck of hoof beats they set out towards Ballyvourney.

CHAPTER SEVENTEEN

Kate Houlihan looked from the castle tower across the lake. She stood above the noise of water and the movement of the road. She wanted a man. The knowledge in the books could not quench the heat burning between her legs. She was as beautiful as they made out, tall, fair haired, milky skin, breasts firm and unused. Her fingers itched at the sandstone of the wall. It was cold. She hitched up her skirts and rubbed her thighs and the velure of her crotch against the stone. Down below her on the road a balladeer stopped. They often did for they knew she loved the songs they wrote for her. He began to sing a new ballad called *Kelly the Man from Mayo.* She wondered who the hero Kelly was. She stood there wondering until night fell. The dog beside her bared its teeth to the wind. The firs on the hillside creaked and water stuttered over the rocks in the stream, complaining.

Mad Houlihan was entombed in the castle. Knitting his hands behind his back, he walked up and down the uneven limestone slabs of his room. His mind was on heraldry, maps, migrations, old names, the bloodstock of men. He was a breeder, bent on mating the best horses, cattle and men. None but royalty would cover Kate and plant her field.

The wilderness about the mountains should be restocked. He would plant trees on the mountains, scour brown rushes from lazy fields, lay roads and walks, raise good cattle on restored land, and the finest child in the continent of Europe would rule over fine acres.

In Galway the Halligans, contained behind bars, went into sober mourning. After a week of talk their father had been sainted, his long life filled with virtue. They would find the plot containing his frail bones and raise the finest tombstone in Connaught to him. He deserved it and would get it. There was no man living but had a good word to say for him for he had never deceived any one in his life. And he would still be alive were it not for the malicious kick that Kelly or one of his lieutenants gave him which rattled his soulcase. But there would be a straightening of accounts one of these days. They would pull the gullet out of him some dark night when he was unwatchful and reeling home drunk. They would jump him from behind a ditch and feed him to the crows.

Judge Hoban, bilious after a bad breakfast, looked down at the frieze of offenders, ragged, rough, red-faced, a knee-bending look in their eyes.

——What's this I hear about plundering graves? he asked Foxy.

——We never took anything but was not our own, Justice, Foxy said.

——Did you know that a corpse was state property like the royal fish?

——I never knew that, Justice, as I'm not well versed in books.

——You disturbed the dead and kept the town awake for a week.

——It was crying we were, Justice, at the sad loss of me father. God rest his soul.

——God rest his soul, they all said, the knee-bending look still in their eyes.

——You gave him little chance of resting. In all my travels up and down the country I never heard of such an offence. There is nothing like it in the books. For sentence, all the men among you will be transported to Sligo Jail for the rest of the summer to break stones. And let it be a warning to you, for I'll have my eye out for you.

——Sligo Jail is a terrible place, Justice, and in foreign parts, Foxy said.

——Silence or you'll spend the winter there too.

The women poured out of the court room and thickened into a pool of wonder in the square. They sent wails to the sky. The curse of Balor was on them ever since the day Caoch Ainsworth sold the false white asses to them. The manacled martyrs were led out bound for Sligo, to eat bitter days housed up from the roads and the small towns and the talk about the fires. The dawn of wonder was only breaking on them when the black Maria was drawn before the court house. It would take them to the station.

—It's more like a hearse than a transporting vehicle, one woman said.

—An awful plague on us and not a man in our beds during the months ahead. It's like a bog without turf.

—Or the sea without salt, another said.

—Or no bird in the sky, added another.

—Or a bramble without a berry, said another still.

They followed the black Maria down the road to the station. They ran along the platform waving at the penitentiary men. The back of the train grew smaller and smaller and disappeared around a bend.

Belmullet paused. It had to. There was enough talk in what happened to fill ten years.

Mickelmas MacLir was locked up in the county home talking and saying things that no normal man would say.

The centre of the town lay charred. The Spanish Ship which had harboured lies and distorted stories for a hundred years was in black ashes. Here and there among the ruins the hoops of barrels stuck out like the ribs of a long carcass. It was all over, what ever had happened, and the wind was taking the ashes down the roads.

Meanwhile Kelly, Faustus MacGinty and Leibide out of Connaught and the darkness and tangle of things made their way from the lonely grave among the Paps, in the direction of Cosruthan. Kelly had made a promise to the poteen maker and now he must keep it. They waked the poteen maker in Ballyvourney in a low, brown raftered shebeen among the Murphys and the O'Donoghues. They were all very solemn as they drank from the barrels of poteen. They talked of serious things; death, love and the dark stairs down to the next life, the coming and going of the sea, the moon going around the earth, the earth going around the sun and of the visible planets, of Kate Houlihan and the nights they would spend with her if they could belt hurley balls down the gullets of the watching wolfhounds.

CHAPTER EIGHTEEN

From the Halls of the Dead the gods looked down at the activities of Kelly and Lubach Caol, the best stallion that ever ate hay in the eternal stables. Bred from an Arabian dam and a Cossack stallion when there was open traffic between the Halls of Life and Death, she had travelled over and back to The Land of the Young twice. Once she had ferried a fool who could not understand that times had changed.

There was divided opinion among them about the advisability of dragging a skinny skitter of a lad back five thousand years to fuddle his brain with insight, and his body with power. One bank of Gods sitting on eternal ditches said that good enough should be left alone. There were enough stories in men's heads that would do until the world split down the seams. The further they grew away from men in time, the more respect for them would grow. Another bank of gods held that the age was sceptical. It had lost the sense of wonder and laughed at the old stories as they would laugh at two lame men in a three-legged race. Another bank argued that the world was like flat dough and needed a stirring of yeast. That there was almost an end to laughter. That life was as dismal as a long wet day and that Kelly was the only man to start a story that would last a thousand years. There was much talk and shuffle during the long eternal evenings as rumours of Kelly floated up through the caves of the dead and out into the asphodel fields.

They followed the progress of Kelly through Belmullet, Louisburgh, Galway and Kerry. They were familiar, the bleak scraps of rocks, the bare mountains, the places through which

Kelly travelled. All the gods were present.

Pantheolon was there, so mystical and forgotten that he was almost transparent.

Dadga and Lug, retired, aching to make ploughs and harrows.

Dadga, as huge as Neifin, sniffed his nose and scratched his danglers. He was the father of three-quarters of them. But his bone and dangler ache had withered. He retained the images of a November night eating gopans of porridge from a cauldron as deep as Lough Ennell, and the tumbles with the Formorian women. He was gross and ugly, pot-bellied and coarse, with hair on his chest like moss on scrub rock.

Lug whittled celestial branches. He was disordered by nerves. His eyes were pouchy from worry. He was everything in his day, carpenter, smith, poet, harper. Too refined for the coarse jokers, he mooned over flowers and watched bees carry honey to the hives. He was tired of the diet of honey and mead.

Oisin was a religious maniac, going around tinkling a cracked bell calling himself to vespers. He carried a big illuminated manuscript from which he would read morning, noon and night.

Finn and his bloated Fenians were there, boasting like retired politicians. They were always retelling the old yarns, and speaking of the days of Howth and hunting on the Central Plain. Lug must have heard the stories eight thousand times, ever since the day they came knocking with blunt spears and dinted shields at the gates of the Halls of the Dead.

——Ah lads, it was one thing we had in our day which is in scarce supply now and that was honesty on our tongues and purity in our hearts, Finn would say.

——That's right, Finn, the soldiers would answer.

——And weren't we the boys that could pull thorns out of the soles of our feet and us running? he would ask again.

——'Tis so and we knew our books of poetry by heart, they added.

——Twelve books. Isn't that so?

——'Tis so.

——We did our bit for Ireland in our day.

—We did.

They were an unpopular group and avoided.

Also there was Manannan Mac Lir, with flowing beard, rusty trident, barnacles on his backside and seaweed in his beard. He smelt of herrings and salt and wandered along the mearing drains of heaven trying to catch a glimpse of the sea. A rotting shipwreck if there ever was one.

The Children of Lir waddled along, never having got the swan out of their nature.

Cuchulainn had carved a hurley out of an ash tree. He spent his day knocking the tops off flowers, aching for a sight of Maeve. She could have every bull in the country if she wished, and he would have driven them down to Connaught himself.

There were hundreds of gods around the Halls of Death, irritating one another, telling the same old stories, for once their term in Ireland was over and they had retired, they had no right to alter any facts in the story of their deeds.

So there was great talk about Kelly. They spent days arguing his relationship, some saying he looked like themselves or their cousins, others saying that he did not belong to that branch of the family at all.

They envied his youth. They envied the legend that was growing up around him. If half of what went on were true, he was better than the best of them and the two idiots that he carried with him would exaggerate his wonders until there would be no ending to them. They all claimed relationship to him.

—If I were asked to swear by the Hill of Tara, Dadga said, I'd say he was carrying every one of my traits. Look at the fine way he has with women. Only to blink at them he has and they run from every corner to him. And a fair hand he is at upending them. By the time he is finished, the country will have the finest crop of bychildren you ever seen. He'll replenish the stock. For if men continue to grow any smaller they will be no bigger than thistles.

But Lug told him to hold his filthy tongue. Kelly was an artist. He had style and flair. The Lug-strain was showing in him. —He's the best harper, fiddler and singer walking the roads of Ireland today.

Manannan Mac Lir recalled his sea play. ——He took to the water like a dolphin as if it were his natural element. Name a god among the whole crowd here who consorted with oily seals and pug-nosed dogfish, who knows the wind directions and the coming and going of the tides, who has oar craft to send him skimming over the waves? You are all inland gods.

Maeve had her eye on him. She would give a lake of virtue to spend a night tossing with him on a feathered bed up at Cruachan. They said that there was a wedge of ice between her thighs. But for all her outward indifference, Kelly was in her mind.

The gods in other meadows heard all the commotions going on among the Irish gods. They came over to the mearing drains and looked into the Celtic plot, chewing Teutonic, Slavonic and Finno -Urgic grass. They chewed and wondered.

——The wild Irish are at it again. When they were not fighting others, they were fighting among themselves.

But they had no idea of what was happening because they could never master the Irish tongue.

CHAPTER NINETEEN

Next morning, Kelly, Faustus and Leibide, scattered of mind
with a wise horse under them, set out in search of the parish
of Cosruthan. Knowing their fragile condition, Lubach Caol
welded them to his sides. He ambled on until he arrived at
the holy well, close to the churchyard and the church of the
parish of Cosruthan. The three dismounted, drank the water
from the well and their heads cleared.

——Now that I see a cross and a statue I'll kneel and say a
prayer for the peaceful rest of my mother's soul that no devil
may lay his black claws on her, Leibide told them.

He knelt on a flagstone, stretched his eyes to heaven like
the saint in the picture, and began directly.

——God . . . I'm no man with words like MacGinty and I
suppose those that have them don't employ them to you.
I'll not bother you too much like a tinker that is always
calling at the house. But in your way around heaven you
might come across one called Nell Ludden from Belmullet.
If there is bog and small fields up there, she's sure to be there
with her own people. She was bad and good. But towards the
end she was very good, so the scales should be in her favour.
She had a great fear of the devil. He has a head like a goat
and burning eyes. Have a look out for her and tell her she had
a good funeral and tell her that I was inquiring about her.
As I said I won't bother you again in a while.

It was spoken in the hearing of Kelly and Faustus. They
did not speak until he was finished. Then they sat down and
took boiled meat from a meat bag and opened a small barrel
of porter. They took the day easy and sat and stared. While

they chewed on meat and time, the parish priest came along.
He was a great scholar in his own way and it was said that he
knew the Latin books backwards. He stopped and looked at
them.

—Travelling I see, he said eyeing them.

—Yes, they answered.

—Have you come a long way?

—We have, father, they answered.

—You are from the west by your voices, he said.

—That's right, father, they replied.

—Three wise men from the west, he remarked, tittering.
Faustus did not like his lack of humility.

—Sure we have no wisdom. All the brains are down in
this part of the country.

—That's true I suppose, the priest said.

—We are only ignorant men, father, and half-lost, Faustus
said.

—You've come a long way.

—We did and we have to go a long way, Faustus said.

—You came on a horse? the priest asked.

—Yes.

—What part of the west?

—Mayo.

—You have mean horses in Mayo. No grass to feed them,
and he laughed in a hard, bitter way at the three strays. They
were as odd as he had seen anywhere.

—Well, you better be careful of yourselves on your travels
for there is a wicked man loose in the country called Kelly
who rides a horse of great magnificence.

—Kelly? they asked.

—Yes. Did you ever hear of him?

—No.

—Everybody has. The saying goes When they heard the
name of Kelly they all flew like midges. He's a despoiler of
women and a deceiver. No village or town is safe from him
and the bishops of Ireland are going to issue a joint letter
banning him from all gatherings.

—Yerra, what would a fellow like that be doing with the
likes of us and we with not a penny between us?

—I thought I'd warn you.

Faustus looked at the book.

—That's a big book you have there, father. You must have great learning.

—That's a Latin book. What book did you reach in school?

—I never went beyond the third book, Faustus said.

—Ah well, some are born to know and others to remain ignorant, the priest told them.

—I'd love to try my hand at reading your book, father, Faustus said.

—If you can make head or tail out of it, I'll give you my trousers, and he handed him the book, upside down. Faustus took it and began reading it as it was handed to him.

—Wait, it's upside down, the priest said.

—That's the way you handed it to me, father, Faustus answered.

—Here, and he gave it to him sideways.

Faustus took the book sideways and began reading.

—It's sideways. Clearly you can make nothing of it, the priest said and he took the book from him.

—I'll tell you, father. Start me off with the first bar and I'll see if I can recite it.

He did.

—Stop, father. Stop. Maybe that's the book I learned from the hedge school master. Does it go anything like this?

Faustus began. The words tumbled out of his mouth. The village, hearing the chanting, came up to the well and gathered about the three figures and the horse. They gazed at the small man who knew all the Latin. The recitation lasted for an hour.

—There you are, father, the first two books and only that my throat is dry and the day hurrying I'd give you the rest.

—You are a wonder and should be up in Dublin at the university.

—I'm an ignorant man who won a priest's trousers.

—But that's only a way of putting things, the priest said.

—That's the way you put it and that's the bet I placed, Faustus said.

—It's blasphemy to take a priest's trousers, a parishioner said.

—He made the bargain and must stand by it, Faustus told them firmly.

The men hushed the womenfolk home, gathered around the priest while he took off his trousers, which were passed over their heads out to Faustus.

—I'll try them on for size later, Faustus told him.

—Bad luck will follow you, somebody said.

But they were up on the horse. They waved the trousers in the air and off they went.

—Do you know who that was father? one of the men asked.

—No.

—Well that was Kelly.

—I hadn't a chance from the word go, the priest moaned.

—He's a danger, but lucky he went or he could have done great damage in the parish.

—In a way it could have been worse. A trousers can be replaced. There are many other things which cannot be replaced, if you get what I mean, father.

—I do. I follow you.

They stood around the parish priest and they all walked together down to his house, so no woman saw him without a trousers.

They went on and on. The horse cantered and there was no rush. At Bothan they met a man with no trousers. He had left it in the back yard of some pub in Macroom and had been so drunk that he could not recall where he had left it. It might not have been in Macroom at all. He had gone into the town late every night, climbing over the back walls and letting himself into the backplaces in search of it.

—What's wrong with you? they asked when they found him cowering behind a ditch.

—You have only to look at me to see what's wrong. I lost me trousers between here and Cork in some backyard and me backside is worn from letting meself down over high walls to retrieve it.

—How long have you been so? Kelly asked.

—A week and a day, he told them.

—You're lucky it's a warm time of year.

—I know. To go unprotected thus in winter would be

the death of me.

He was a small, meagre man. The look in his face told them that he possessed ten acres, five of them bog.

—I'm tired days sleeping behind ditches and haybarns, and nights going from town to town, me backside bare.

—And why not get the tailor to make you a trousers?

—Sure there was five years wearing in the other one. 'Twould be extravagant to do so, and it only dislocated somewhere.

Faustus took the priest's trousers from inside Leibide's shirt. —There try it for size, and he threw it down to him.

The little man jumped into it and it bloomed about him. —Sure it's a grand size surely, he said, tying it double around him, it fits like a glove.

—Are you sure it doesn't tickle you under the armpits? Kelly asked.

—No, it's a grand size. Made for me. It's the black colour that worries me. 'Tis like something the bishop would have on.

—Worry not. Black is in fashion now and by a law of Queen Victoria everybody will soon be walking the roads in black trousers, Kelly assured him.

—Well, it's grand to be first in the fashion, the little man said.

—There you are now. They won't know you when you walk in at home.

—I'll surprise them all.

He did. And ever afterwards he was called Johnny the Priest.

The promise fulfilled to the poteen maker, they headed east along the coast. They passed over mountains, streams, through private domains, meadows, woods. They passed Dungarvan, Waterford, Cheekpoint, Wexford, Arklow, Wicklow, until the walls of the Wicklow Mountains appeared before them.

—Well, Leibide, I always promised you I'd show you China and we are approaching China now. So keep your eyes peeled. These are the Mountains of Mongolia and if you look east you'll see the China sea.

——I knew it was a long way off, Kelly, but I never thought it was this far.

——It's far indeed and the people living in China are as different from us as goats are from cows, Kelly told them.

From Three Rock Mountain they looked down on Dublin city; the dog head of Howth sniffing the sea. Kingstown with granite paws about a litter of ships: spires prodding the sky.

——It's as big nearly as the eye can see. There must be close on a thousand people down there and no chance of them ever getting to know one another, Leibide said.

——It's very big. We'll look at the monuments and if we like the place stay on for awhile.

Their approach was noted. The seismograph in Rathfarnham Castle was moidered by galloping horse reverberations, tittering the instruments. Father Felucius Green had spent three nights and days looking at the progression of the local earthquake. It was like drums beating for war. Yet the city was solid. Nelson's pillar had not toppled. The obelisk in the Phoenix Park stood square and solemn, recording battles. It could be a storm at sea he reflected. Then again it might not. It could be a supernatural misunderstanding. Then again it might not.

They rode into the city. They went unnoticed. They passed through Stephen's Green, Fitzwilliam Square, past the Bank of Ireland, down Sackville Street and turned towards the Phoenix Park.

——It's a hostile place, Kelly remarked.

——I wish I were among my own, Leibide said.

——I feel the cold in my uppers, Kelly said, it's time we headed back to where we came from.

They turned the horse in the Lucan direction and kept going west until they crossed the Shannon. The air was fresher. The water flowed with music. Autumn had matured the bogs.

CHAPTER TWENTY

Robert Orthega Bollingbrook, pock scorched, exhausted,
left the bawdy house, sniffed the vomit of a low tide, made
his way across the tinkling morning cobblestones and entered
his waiting carriage. It listed on exhausted springs. The
wheels moved slowly across the metal road and he fell asleep.

He was Irish, Spanish, English. The clear breed showed in
the family records. The blood was blue as far back as it went.
The blue blood was now carried across the Liffey by way of
Butt Bridge in the direction of Kingstown. The blue blood
coursed slowly about the wobbly corpus, netted by purple
corrupted veins. His face sagged and bleached, was loose on
bone structure and drooped under his ears and chin. He was
getting old. Blue blood had abused its privilege and now some
villain asp from the bilge water of a strange ship had poisoned
him. It had invaded his system and fattened on good meat
and wine. His dishevelled dreams stirred up mud. The dome
of his head towering above him pressed down its bone scope.

Irish and Spanish and English. His monogrammed history
was embroidered on his silk underwear, a thing for which the
whore in the bawdy house had little respect. ──Money on
the nail, she said before the transaction.

──The graciousness has gone from life, were the only
words he could find as he handed over the money.

──I suppose I'll have to take off your trousers for you, she
said, looking at his corpus.

──Yes. Little attentions like that would be appreciated, he
said.

──I should charge you more, sir. This is all above the call

of duty.

It had been a haggle. Changing one's custom is unpleasant.
But then he had an outstanding debt with Titty Lilly. He was
nearly broke. On bleary nights, sitting before his Adam's
fireplace, he looked at the flames eating at his substance.
There was little gold left in the Robert Orthega Bollingbrook
coffers. Letters to Spain and England and visits to Irish
relations had brought bland refusals. There was no ore left in
their veins. He pondered by instinct. He saw his house,
horses, whores, silks, burn before him. He cast around for
answers. Only one answer came to him. He would have to go
to stud. There was many a family could be replenished with
blue blood. But maybe he carried idiocy and poison now.
The foreign ship's bilge asp was fermenting under his skin. It
was boring into bone and marrow. It would eat the sanity
from his spine. No ointment could be diked against it. The
broken banks had been filled too often. The roars of a mad
uncle, strapped in an iron strait-jacket, sounded in his ear.
Donna Connor Orthega lying in the cathedral of Seville
would be ashamed of him. He pulled across the curtains of
his carriage and looked at the dawn movement of the streets,
at the strand at Sandymount and the waves coming ashore
regularly, after a sober night.

He saw rats at Blackrock and pounded at them with his
stick. But they split and formed again, propagated, sulked,
mimicked him, exposed fine white teeth.

—Oh rats are eating up the world, he roared, rats, rats,
rats. An ancestor conquered the sea and brought gold from
Mexico. I cannot clear this plague from my feet. Where is
the piper who can charm these pests away?

The carriage driver, dead to the roars, drove with civility
through the streets, for nobility has its obligations and so
has its lackey. He pulled aside the curtain and looked out. He
saw death's horse itself, chewing a skull-like turnip, clobber
down the civil streets of Blackrock like a barbarian in Rome,
thin, meagre, bent, spavined. It could have been the starved
horse of the Apocalypse. On his back he carried a fool, a
dwarf, a man with red hair and a shining eye. The world was
falling apart and phantoms and phantasms were loose in
the streets.

Finally his carriage wheels crunched on a laundered drive. Civilized silence and Spanish iron-work, softened by ordered roses, greeted him. Fat, full, faltering, fired with foreign crabs, he was supported out of his carriage. He dragged his wobbling carcass up steps through an ante-chamber and into the presence of Mad Houlihan standing severe, febrile, nervous before the Adam's mantlepiece.

——Houlihan, he said, what are you doing here at this hour of the morning, when any decent rake should be in bed?

Houlihan bowed to the bloated feet of Robert Orthega Bollingbrook. Awe and reverence stiffened his jaw when he thought of the genealogical network of copulations which had gone into the creation of the tub of grave fodder in front of him.

——I had no intention whatsoever of disturbing you like this, and he galloped after the heels of the nobility around the room, but I came to speak with you concerning the prospects of Kate, my daughter, for a father wishes only the best for his daughter.

——True, Houlihan, but we are men of the world and I must ask you if you have considered my terms.

——All you asked for at our last meeting. Wide land in Connaught, rich in milk cows. Mountains with sheep, wine from Spain, a castle above the Corrib, the rent of five hundred small farmers, the lord's right, and eighty kegs of gold.

——My service is surely worth more than eighty kegs of gold. Two hundred kegs, man. It is rumoured that the vaults of your castle are heaped with Spanish sovereigns.

——Ah sure my lord, 'tis only rumours. I'm a poor man making overtures in the interest of my daughter.

——A lady no man has seen but by report. Maybe I'm to marry a worn out hag, Bollingbrook said.

——But the fame of Kate's beauty is a proverb. It is sung about in ballads, and her learning and sweet talk is without equal if you were to roam the towns of Ireland. She would charm the anger from a sultan as the lady did in the tale. And the way into her is guarded by virtue and vigilance, and the locks and doors of the castle.

——Two hundred kegs of gold.

——A hundred and twenty.

——A hundred and eighty.

——A hundred and sixty.

——A hundred and sixty.

They clasped hands and Kate was sold.

Houlihan, drunk on the thought of blood, looked at the figure which carried the best blood in Europe. If he could get a stir from him and him wedged between Kate's legs, then he would have captured the best stallion in the park lands of the continent.

——And when can I meet with your daughter, Kate? Robert Orthega Bollingbrook asked.

——I will pay all the gold necessary to bring you west into the Corrib country, for it is suitable that you should cap and kindle her in the land that's coming to you, that cows might have better calfs, horses good foals, women strong children and autumn crops.

——Well we'll see about replenishing the stock. In November I'll travel slowly to the Corrib country with my retinue. Have the field ready for planting.

——I warrant I will.

He had cemented the bargain. He left the room, mounted his horse and headed west along the canal.

Robert Orthega Bollingbrook, looking at a canvas of a bright, controlled English landscape above the fire, wished that his pleasure lay east in England and not among the cold stones of the west. But the blight of bad times and the debts in his bones had to be paid. He was the father only of a crop of bastards, which carried no maker's name and was condemned to the obscurity of narrow streets. It was time to raise a crop of wheat. His flesh quivered when he thought of the discomforts of a stony castle, the bleak lake, scabby mountains. But he could not escape his obligation to propagate.

A gallery of portraits, which mounted the marble stairs with him, screamed that they needed offspring; demanded that face and feature should be carried on. There they stood, firm, resolute eyes following him about the house. Their bones lay in monumental tombstones across Europe, in the warm convents of Spain, under the domes of great churches

in Italy, quiet in green plots in England. He was the confluence of all these streams, the river in which the strains
met.

He felt his flesh loose about him like clumsy clothes. He
mounted the stairs, passed the censure of faces, followed by
his footman. Under warm sheets he forgot Mad Houlihan
and his daughter Kate.

CHAPTER TWENTY-ONE

November stood about the Shannon. There was a hard edge
on the wind. It whittled small waves off the river, raked old,
eccentric leaves into odd corners, where they huddled like
small women in a county home. Trees, picked, stood charred
against the sky, like pressed specimens, black netted veins on
maroon evenings.

Autumn was dead.

When Kelly passed across the Shannon he knew that he
had to leave Leibide and Faustus. Now they would be
welcome in small towns which in one way or another were
obligated to them. They carried the story with them. It
would grow and branch. His immortality depended on them.

The old horse was jaded, the magic berries had lost their
virtue. Life was thin in stone, tree, animal, man. The towns
were drawing in the limits of their landscapes. Talk was
gapped. Isolation thickened between esker ridges. Few went
into exile from the small stations. Coltsfoot, hoofgreen, grew
in hedges and mouldering houses, in neglected orchards
beside gnawed windfalls. Pincher frost cut finely. It was the
month before December.

They rode on, the horse panting through scroffy phlegm.
Their heads drooped. No talk knitted. Heads half listed in
sleep. Listless mouths. Lids sealing. Slatecold sky. A network of limestone walled fields. Nibbled sheep grass. Sere
rushes in careless fields, comatose woods, knobby with
mystery. Famished cattle, the cold wind carving substance
from them. Houses on hills hostile. Thin sunlight casting
morgue shadows.

——All our days seem dead, Kelly, Faustus said, perhaps we are weary worn out, looking for somewhere to bed down for the winter. The days are getting cold now and there isn't much colour in the sky. The colour in everything has faded.

They looked at the dead land.

——I can't understand, Kelly. You're the one man I thought could stand against all the desolation. Sure there is none better than you for the song and the dance and courting a woman when the humour is on you.

——There are times when I'm a stranger to myself, Faustus. But I seem to die with the year. Maybe it is something that is in me locked to everything that is growing.

——You are not going into a cave and sleeping the winter away like the northern bears? Faustus asked.

——It's much more than that but I can't phrase it properly.

——There is nothing to raise you out of your bad spirits? Faustus asked.

——One woman.

——Kate Houlihan?

——Yes. I have heard so much of her beauty that I can't sleep nights thinking about her. It's like setting out in a ship for the golden fleece.

——But it might be the illusion of pedlars, the dreams we build to keep life and heart in us.

——But you know of the search, Faustus. You have spent your life looking for it.

——It's a swamp, Kelly.

——I have looked at the blue veins under the clear skin of women, and felt them under me. But always I was thinking of the thighs of Kate Houlihan, kissing her stiff breasts, feeling her nipples hardening and knowing the love tangle of her limbs.

——You're looking for the flesh of the world, Kelly. No woman under the sun can give that much.

——She can, Faustus. This is the one field in which I want to cut the deep earth. Don't you know my need?

——There is no need between my legs.

——It's beyond all painful blisters, wounds or hunger, Kelly said.

——You are not the man, Kelly, that we met the un-

comfortable wet day in Belmullet, when we never needed the
sunshine to warm us. It's all before you, Kelly. Surely you
are not growing old?

—I'm as old as all the monuments of Ireland.

—And where is the laughter?

—Gone too.

—It's asleep inside you. It will quicken again in spring.

—There is no knowing.

The horse hobbled along the road.

—Kelly, Leibide said, the hunger is eating me inside. It's
like I've never been fed before in my life. I feel weakness
coming on me and blackness at the back of my head.

—The next town we see, we'll stop and have something to
eat and drink, Kelly told him.

They saw a small town among trees. A Protestant tower
and a Catholic steeple raised themselves up from the roots of
graves above house roofs. A humped bridge led into the
market crotch and a still mill-wheel shredded race water.
They stopped before a public house, dismounted and went
inside.

—Is that your horse at the door? the landlady asked.

—Yes.

—Well, she's the worst nag I've ever seen come across the
bridge and if she is any sign of the gold in your pocket, we
want no trucking with you here.

—Would you like to see the colour of my money? Kelly
asked.

—I would as you are strangers here.

He took a handful of gold and scattered it across the
counter. —Gold from California and Klondyke.

It slithered and twinkled across the counter like fish from
a net.

—Glory be to God but it's not robbers you are, after
killing? she asked.

—No, but honest men.

Her husband ran in from the kitchen when he heard the
sound of gold, bit at the pieces, became obsequious.

—Anything in the house gentlemen, any command will
be carried out, he said.

Kelly pushed him the gold.

—Take it and leave us in peace until we call. We want bed and board for a week.

—I'll lock the door and you can have the place to yourselves, and the back is out through the kitchen, the wife told them.

—Right.

—I suppose you heard the news? the man asked.

—What news?

—There is great talk of the journey of Robert Orthega Bollingbrook through Ireland. He's a great Dublin gentleman and he is coming this way. It was brought by the post.

—And what would he be doing in the country at this time of year? Kelly asked.

—To marry Kate Houlihan, the daughter of Mad Houlihan, if all that we hear is right. She is the great beauty they all speak of and he's a great gentleman.

—So Venus is to mate with Vulcan, Kelly said.

—No, but a Dublin gentleman called Mr. Bollingbrook from Dublin is to wed Kate Houlihan, he repeated.

—Bring me drink and bring me food and leave us to our troubles, Kelly roared and they ran from the room.

He sat in despair, wrapped in silence.

A plan formed in his mind and he began to laugh.

Kelly was laughing again.

He sang for them, and recited long poems he had composed. They talked until it was late into the night. They drank and talked for five nights and five days. Faustus and Leibide were reeling drunk when it was finished.

—Well it's time for us to go our separate ways, Kelly told them.

—You're having us on, Kelly. Sure we would travel with you until time runs out, Faustus told him.

—Well, it can't be like that. You have seen all that's in the nature of man to see and you have done more laughing than a townland would do in a hundred years, Kelly told them.

—Indeed we have, Faustus said.

—Well, as all good and bad things come to an end, so our travelling must.

Leibide bent his head and sobbed, as he had sobbed at his mother's funeral.

——We'll never forget you, Kelly, and all of Ireland will hear of your great deeds, Leibide said.

——You know you will be welcome in all the small towns. And while you have the story to tell, there will be food and shelter for you, Kelly told them both.

It was time to go.

They were drunk when he led them on to the square. Leibide took Faustus and put him up on his shoulders. Faustus, with his feet around Leibide's neck and his hands about his forehead, looked out over the world. Now they were a reasonable man.

Leibide staggered across the bridge, turned around at the hump and Faustus waved goodbye. They walked down into November, bearing the story with them.

He loosed Lubach Caol, hit him on the rump and left him to drag his way out of the town. ——Come back again when you are needed, he told him. They were all gone like a forgotten conversation. He went indoors and waited for Robert Orthega Bollingbrook.

CHAPTER TWENTY-TWO

The long cavalcade moved across the country, horsemen, servants, baggage. They rested in the towns and moved through November at an easy pace. Everywhere Robert Orthega Bollingbrook stayed the leading families came to him and paid their respect and homage. He was fated and feasted like the Queen of Sheeba, and his presence did great honour to all occasions.

His fastidious palate found only ashes and vinegar in the large houses, but as a lord down on his luck he had to stifle his fine tastes. So he smiled and wiped his nose with a silken handkerchief.

They rested for a night at Tuam, which was two days journey from Houlihan's castle. It was a night of music, food and wine, as all the other nights had been. The lords of Connaught were in attendance. They came from Sligo, Leitrim, Roscommon, Mayo and Galway in their finery and with their eligible daughters. Under candelabras of old Waterford glass they danced to the strains of the waltz. The scene reminded them of the pump room in Bath and days in London.

Robert Orthega Bollingbrook always sat at the head of the table, bored yet condescending, nodding this way and that as etiquette indicated. The finest ladies in the province were introduced to him. He spoke some inane words to them which they cherished and remembered when Queen Victoria was an old and stubby queen, hay-cocked shaped.

There was an undercurrent of criticism behind ladies' fans. They remarked that Houlihan was a vulgar name, as was the name Kate. They asked where did she come from and, replying to their own questions, said that she came from common Irish stock. Was it true that she was locked in a fortress by a barbarian father? Yes, the old order of things was changing. And was not Robert Orthega Bollingbrook such a fine, handsome fellow? His family was one of the most distinguished in Europe and he had links with the ancient Caesars.

It was a gracious night at Tuam. Nowhere in Ireland was there a more refined assembly or more delicate blood. The inhospitable landscape of bog and rush and stone was a thousand miles away outside the town.

Out of this inhospitable landscape of bog and rush and stone came O'Leary the Harper, his wild harp slung behind him. He carried a patch over his eye and felt awkward in the town of Tuam. He met a rambling drunkard who directed him to the great house.

——All the nobility of Europe are gathered there tonight and there is a ton of silver on the tables and strange boomeranged fruit. It's the talk of Connaught, this wedding, he said, pointing in the direction of the great house.

O'Leary the Harper made his way further into the town, found the great house and heard the mid-European music. Knowing his station, he went around to the back of the great house and knocked at the scullery door. A scullery maid answered.

——Who are you? she asked, looking at the strange figure.

——O'Leary the Harper. I thought the master might have employment for me. I play the harp, juggle and put riddles to people.

——Away with you. The people up in the great hall are of the finest quality. Nobody wishes to hear Irish harpers on a night like this.

——Well you won't refuse me a bite to eat or if you do I'll put a curse on you. I have great curses and they never fail to work.

She let him in and he sat down at the huge kitchen table and ate the leavings of the quality. While he was eating, the major-domo rushed into the kitchen in some confusion.

——It seems that our guest, the right honourable Robert Orthega Bollingbrook, is wearied of the orchestra. They only know nine waltzes and they have played them in every house he visited. He is visibly bored.

It was then his eyes rested on O'Leary the Harper, his wild harp resting at the wall. He was a strange creature and the cloak he wore stranger still. It was yellow, saffron, red, green, purple and amber like a stained glass window faded with wind and rain. His jerkin was of oily leather, stained and shiny, his breeches rough as meal sacking, bound to his calves with sugan ropes. He was a ludicrous figure, and, knowing that kings once had fools, the major-domo thought that Harper O'Leary might entertain the gentry.

——Can you play the harp? he asked.

——Some days I'm sweet and some days I'm sour. Harps have humours, but tonight I'm in great fettle.

——And what else can you do?

——I juggle and put riddles to people.

——Can you entertain quality?

——I can.

——Well come then and I'll announce you.

He followed the major-domo up a back stairs, his wild harp slung behind him, and then they went up another stairs and along a corridor and then out into a main hall, where candelabras clustered like galaxies above him and the walls were lined with portraits. The major-domo disappeared for a moment and then reappeared.

——I have to give you an introduction. What can I say about you?

O'Leary the Harper milked information concerning himself from the lobe of his ear. Then he said, ——Tell them that I'm the last of the old Irish harpers and that I learned the harp from Harper Dowd who learned it from Carolan himself.

——That should do, the major-domo said and he threw open wide doors and in a loud voice introduced Harper O'Leary. He rushed back and said ——You're on. This is your big chance.

——I'll do my best. I'm badly in need of a break.

The major-domo pushed him forward into the luxury of lights and heat and the odour of clean bodies. The smell of fine food filled his lungs. There was much laughter when the Harper appeared. It was not lost on him. Immediately he did a comical jig on the centre of the floor. They liked his dance. He did it again. Robert Orthega Bollingbrook slipped from his satin chair onto the floor with laughter and was dragged back into position by two servants.

Harper O'Leary then played on the harp, badly and deliberately and pretended he could not understand why they laughed. Then he played sad, sweet music and when they were crying, he pretended that he could not understand why they were not laughing.

Later he went through his riddle routine and very few could follow the complexities and tangles. So, seeing that they were stupid and in order not to offend the quality, he did his little comical jig and they were greatly pleased.

He had crowned their night with laughter. Robert Orthega Bollingbrook was greatly pleased at the whole show and said he would retain him under contract. He would come to the marriage and entertain the guests with some new routines. This pleased O'Leary the Harper very much.

He slept that night in the cellar of the great house and next morning he joined the cavalcade and moved west to the Corrib country.

CHAPTER TWENTY-THREE

News of Kate Houlihan's marriage spread like gorse fire across mearing drains in July. There was no tether to the talk in market, pub or church door. Kate was getting married to the finest blood in the land. Well, it would put an end to the talk and the stories. Walled in by marriage, worn by carrying, the stricture about not desiring another man's wife would put an end to her beauty. No ballad man ever sang of a married woman. Maybe because their imaginations stood a chance with a woman whose apple has not been plucked. But the memory of the woman she was in her youth would last like the standing stones, when the flesh had rotted from all their bones.

It would be a great day in the sprawling village of Poll Dubh under the castle, if the wind did not come too hard, or the rain fester beyond the mountains. Tinkers, trick-of-the loops, card sharpers, ribbon vendors, pilferers, fortune tellers, thimble riggers, butchers, stall keepers, fiddlers, black toothed rhymers were gathering from the far limits of the provinces. There was never going to be a day like the day of the marrying of Kate Houlihan. It would be a fair, a pattern, a holiday mixed in one; a day for the annalists.

Foxy Halligan would be there. He had erected a tombstone over his father's grave. It had cost fifteen pounds. He had haggled with the mason, knocking him down from twenty-five pounds. Devil a one would know that Foxy Halligan or his father were tinkers when they looked at the inscription. Foxy had no idea what age Angel was when he died, so he settled on the round number of sixty as it was easy to carve. Not that the exact year was important. Sixty was near enough and if Angel was not sixty he should have been.

——Make it in big letters, sir, Foxy said, for from what I see too much space goes to waste on tombstones. I want everyone passing the road in a cart to see me father's name standing out remarkable.

——There are limits, the mason told him, you must balance your spaces. You don't want a shop sign above your father.

——Well I wanted it bigger than newspaper print. Two hands high about. And put me down, one hand high, for erecting it. He'll know I didn't forget him when the final day comes for emptying the graves.

——That's a long way off, the mason said.

——No matter. Dublin is a long way off and you can get there if you set out at the beginning of the month. So come it must as every Sunday comes.

——I suppose you're right, the mason said.

——And I'll build a wall around it three hands high, to keep out the wind on lonesome nights.

——That will cost five pounds extra.

——Two.

——Nothing less than three pounds.

——Two pounds ten.

——Two pounds ten.

——Put it there.

They spat on their hands and cemented their bargain with spittle.

Foxy had great accounts of Sligo jail. The walls were half as high as Croagh Patrick and kept out the sun most of the day. He had been manacled to a wall with an iron chain and the rust had reddened his wrist and got into his blood. He had met men there who had murdered their wives, mothers, and brothers for acres of land. Others were chained to the wall because they had stolen sheep. There was a black man from Africa, Paudie Coola, a sailor, who had tumbled a girl from Sligo and got her with a brown child. Fellows had been flogged with the cat of nine tails until their backs were like potato drills. And they all had ate yellow buck from a trough like pigs. He painted a black picture of the grey walls and the big wooden door with the small barred windows and the stern guards. —I declare, it was worse than Hell itself and many a good man died in there from severity and the want of light.

The thought of the two months in jail brought back the name Kelly. A curse on him, but they had not had a lucky day since they tangled with him in Belmullet. But they would have the measure of him the next time they met. They would tear the eyes out of his head.

—And now the talk has it that we ran from him like midges, Foxy told them.

—He's a shocking man to have anything to do with. A carrier of the plague and best left severely alone, one of the Halligans said.

—That's weak talk. We weren't organized then but the next time we will be like a military battalion going off east.

Mad Houlihan's eyes were bright with ambitious delight when he started up the curling stone stairs that led to Kate's room. Every step reminded him of the care he took in mating and breeding. He had an eye for quality in a beast. Was not Kate's mare, Bawn, the finest of her breed? A lifetime of choice until Carro had dropped her from Mask on a New Year's morning.

The sun was edging down behind the mountains. A scimitar of moon brightened in the east. It was a burnt, amber evening, quiet as a tranquil mind.

Kate stood on the balcony outside her room, looking over the world. The books had turned to ashes in her library ever since she had heard ballad singers singing of Kelly. She was tired of the prattle of old women, the sniffing of senile teachers. Kate wanted a man. There was a fire between her legs like a luxurious itch. She rubbed her thighs against the stonework, trying to cool its hot tongue. She cried out against the silk evening. No spirited animal should be kept in a stall she thought and fields breaking into flower. She heard Mad Houlihan turning the key in the heavy door. If she had a knife she would castrate him good and proper.

—Come and close the window, Kate, and sit down until we have a good talk.

She sat in an ornate armchair, composed herself and listened. Mad Houlihan hopped up and down the room on his bad leg. His mind was racing so fast that he forgot to talk. Then he broke out.

—Kate, I have great news for you.

She held her silence.

—Well you know yourself that you come from great stock. The Houlihans go back as far as the first man who set foot in this land and it is reputed that he was a god from the shores of the Mediterranean sea. So it's only right that the best should mate with the best, for were it not so your mare Bawn would only be a horse in men's minds. It's the same with people of blood. And you, Kate, are not like the men and women who meet at crossroads and tumble on cocks of hay. Kate, you are going to marry the best man in Ireland in a week's time. The seal and guarantee has been set on the bargain.

—And what about picking my own man? she said.

—Your choice has always been mine, Kate, and that's the way it's going to be.

—But I want to marry a man I love.

—You do in my backside. I have the eye for the quality and you will be led and said by me.

—Not unless he has the measure of me.

—You'll marry and like it.

—I won't.

Fury boiled inside him.

—This is what you were born for. This is the reason I bought the best masters in the country to this room, to drag you up from the gutter. Marry you will.

—And who have you picked for me?

—The noblest man in Ireland. Robert Orthega Bolling-brook. Not only the finest man in Ireland but in Europe. No more suitable mate is drawn in a carriage through the cities.

—And what age is he?

—A suitable age. He is within a week of the castle. So it is time you prepared to meet him. We will start the celebrations when he arrives and they will run for a week.

—And what if I don't marry him?

—Marry him you will or I'll drive you from the castle

naked to wander around the world, where you could not feed or dress yourself and you with rich wants.

He left the room, closed the door and walked to the landing. He opened another secret door and went inside. It was a small, unknown room. He pulled back a small shutter and looked down on the large double bed. He closed the shutter, chuckled and walked away. Mating had to be supervised.

Kate sat blank with horror. And then she fell to thinking. Any man is better than no man and it is equal when you are in the dark. And marry she must. It was better than being a pickled spinster. The reason had its reason that the heart could never understand.

So the best seamstresses were called from Galway. They lodged in the castle and stitched and cut and stitched and cut during the nights and the days until they had a dress of gold and white ready for her. And the artists and artisans fashioned the bridal chamber and hung tapestries on the walls. The soft down of geese-padded mattresses and pillows, and the sheets were of silk. On the floor lay the white fleece of sheep for her feet. Each evening she sat and wondered about the man who was coming the length of Ireland to marry her.

Excitement fermented in Poll Dubh. They looked up from the village at the square tower, tall and wide, where Kate Houlihan lived. And their eyes passed to the trees on the mountainsides covered with walks, walled in from the grousy heather. Across the mountain Kate had rode Bawn, her white veils flying, two cossack soldiers riding beside her. Now she was ready for the marriage bed, primed like a peacock for a king's garden. Coloured stalls were sprouting up in the triangular market place. The travelling players had built a small stage of wooden planks on porter barrels, the end curtained off from the actors. Mag Bourke had scrubbed the chairs and the tables of her eating house, so that a man would see his face or bum in them, and the cauldron, big as a cock of up-turned hay, was stocked with faggots ready for firing. Salted pigs heads and crubeens were lodged in the settle bed for the day of the wedding. Flags fluttered from the house and bunting dipped from chimney to chimney. All classes of low men mixed in the market place. They were the familiar faces from the fairs, the racecourses and the small circuses. Already the countryside was congregated in the long wobble of street, going from stall to stall, waiting for the arrival of the great man from Dublin.

The Halligans arrived in their caravans, leading piebald horses, asses and goats into the street. They were the laughing stock of the crowd for every ballad singer in the country was singing about them. They were moody, silent, huddled.

And the story of Kelly was on every tongue.

—It is said by reliable witnesses that half the women in Ireland have been under him and his appetite for them is larger than Big Ugly Connor's for potatoes. And the same women are mad for him, even the respectable ones that have standing with people. He has only to blink an eye and their skirts are up, an old man said to a friend, and their heads over pints.

—In a fight he'd ate ten men. Sure look at the Halligans and the change that came over them. There's not a solid man among the whole lot of them. And the kick he gave old Halligan in the arse twisted his guts that he tangled inwardly and not a bit of food would lodge in his belly until the day he died in Galway, his friend answered back.
him even if they have to spend every hungry years of their lives following him up and down the country, the old man said.

—He must be a great man to know and more than of natural proportions, his friend commented.

—So tall they say that he could ate hay out of a loft. Sure the two that travelled with him on the magic horse of his say he's not normal at all, but one of the gods you could hear the old men talking about, come back again.

—Them's the two fellows that are welcome in every town. The big fellow with no brains at all and the other who has all the brains and no size and reputed to be the smallest man in Ireland.

—Them's the two. They are the only ones to know the whole story.

—It would be great to have them a night by the hearth, saying it all out as they saw it happen.

The talk in Poll Dubh had no end. But there was a gap of silence as the town gawked at the arrival of Robert Orthega Bollingbrook. The long train of travellers passed through the town coach by coach. Not only the travellers from Dublin but the grand people from all quarters of Ireland who had joined the cavalcade on the way. Silk and satins and the tinkle of silver bells and coaches as long as six ass carts and high as a reek of turf. And every coach had a retinue of servants, done out in wigs and velvet, and serious as marble statues.

Robert Orthega Bollingbrook sat in the first carriage, curtained from the curious eyes. There was no knowing what type of gentleman he was.

There were many queer ones among the cavalcade which passed through Poll Dubh, but none as queer as the harper with the patch over his eye. He was dressed in all colours of the rainbow with a bag slung over his shoulder and a harp under his elbow.

—A copper for a tune, somebody called after him, but he looked ahead and did not say a word.

—Declare but how did he get into such company? somebody asked.

—Maybe he's a great man with his fingers. Some have it in the fingers like the Fiddler Rafftery.

Through the silent village the wheels creaked, the shod horses tapped, and out again and up to the great gate of the castle. It opened, swallowed them up and the gap of silence in the village fell in. The courtyard circled with activity. Mad Houlihan opened the door of the coach and out stepped Robert Orthega Bollingbrook.

CHAPTER TWENTY-FOUR

He stood puddle broad in the courtyard, pouchy eyes pawing at the ground, afraid of the cold fortress. His mind darted to the city comforts of Dublin, streets ending at copper cupolas above Greek fronts, or lines of trees in parks leading to manageable hills. The crowd swarmed about him, twittering like gossipy swallows. Tired, aimless, he was led away by Mad Houlihan, through vaulted passages into a large room with heavy furniture.

——Welcome to my castle, your lordship, Mad Houlihan said.

——Wine, man, and let me hear the ring of your gold, and give me the sight of the woman I have come to marry.

——In what order, sir?

——In the order of my words.

Mad Houlihan rang a thick bell. A servant in awkward lavender breeches came to the door.

——Murtagh, wine for the fine gentleman.

——What colour, sire? Red, yellow or white?

——The wine from Spain, you fool.

The wine was brought, poured and sipped. While Bollingbrook rolled the chilled wine in his jowls and twisted the cut glass to various lights, the gold was rolled across the floor in kipper-curing barrels, scattered on the flags to make sure it did not contain turnips and shovelled back again by the two greatest fools in Connaught. They did not know the value of the gold, except that they could roll about on the mountains heaped in the cellars. They kept a firm guard on it. For this service they were given bed and board, and the big pies the women in the kitchen made for them from rhubarb. They carried the barrels away.

—The woman now that so much is spoken and written about, Robert Orthega Bollingbrook said.

—Remember, sir, she is a lady of haughty temperament, and not as easily handled as gold.

—Did I come a hundred and fifty coach miles to meet a haughty, wayward shrew? I like my meat cooked, tender, submissive, when I put a fork in it.

—Oh she's well cooked. No finger woman was ever served on the table of any man's bed, Mad Houlihan said.

—I hear nothing but talk. Bring the woman before me and we'll put her through her paces.

Kate had looked down into the village for a week. Now it was a mass of changing colours and movement. She was above all this. From now on she would wear a hard mask. It must hide her feelings. She would marry and mate. That was the hard order of things. Nobility had its obligations to breed clean offspring, to drop women who could take men and fences at a stride, eat from silver plates and order servants, and men handsome and distinguished. She followed the coaches through the streets, up to the castle, carrying the stallion to stud. An old crooked-nosed crone knocked at her door and came in. Kate sat before her mirror combing her hair.

—The great man from Dublin would like to see you, she told her.

Robert Orthega Bollingbrook drank his wine slowly and waited. Mad Houlihan limped up and down the floor impatiently, kneading his nervous hands. There was a sound of slippers on the stairs and Kate walked into the room. Robert Orthega Bollingbrook had seen nothing like her on the grand tour, or the tour he had made into Russia, or in the high and low places in London, Glasgow, Belfast, and Dublin. Gold would not buy her. She had the close breeding of five hundred years in her nostrils alone and the prodding breasts. A man could splay her waist with his fingers. Hips and buttocks did not carry common fat.

Kate, firm and taut as a Greek statue, looked at the wallet of slobbery fat, bagged in silk, the belly of sensual living under his chin. She had a wish to vomit. He was already twitching for her. He would roll her on the floor if he could pull his backside from the maw of the chair. His imagination was sniffing about her, nosing her buttocks, crotch, tits, like a skulking dog about a bitch.

—You called me, sir, she said.

—I wished to see you, he said.

—Look at me, and she turned around.

—My dear Kate, he wishes to know you.

—I know what the bugger wants. I can see it in his goat eyes.

—Hold your bitter tongue, daughter, Mad Houlihan roared.

—I'll say what's on my mind. Look at the slobber on his mouth. Do you expect me to lie under a heap of lard like that?

—Stop, girl, I say.

—Would you close your mouth? You won't have to carry that weight of belly on top of you, or fill your lungs with the stench of his teeth or have his hands slobbering you like a baker slapping and kneading dough. I'll mate with him once a year when I'm ripe and nothing more over against that.

But Robert Orthega Bollingbrook, mesmerised like a rabbit by her beauty, did not hear a word she spoke.

—Leave now, Mad Houlihan ordered, and we'll meet at the feast I'm giving.

She left. Robert Orthega Bollingbrook woke from his reverie.

—It's a bargain, he said.

—So let it be, Houlihan said.

—You will come to the feast tonight? Mad Houlihan asked.

—Yes, he replied.

CHAPTER TWENTY-FIVE

There was a mad order in the feast. Houlihan himself moved between kitchen and hall commanding servants. The tables stood under one ceiling on two levels. In the upper half, reserved for the grand people, candelabras sparkled. The tables stood around an open space which was to be used for music and entertainment. The lower level was like a dark theatre. Tables were close together without linen or light. It was traditional in the big house to invite servants, herdsmen, carpenters, masons, tailors, cobblers and tinkers to wedding feasts. A thousand were gathered into the courtyard and rooms as the sun went down. People were called by a servant and their position was taken according to their dignity or age. Foxy Halligan and some of his tribe were at the end of the room near the door. They looked up at the lighted level of the room, the tables weighed down with old wine and new food. There was great expectation and talk of Kate Houlihan. So much was said about her, that it seemed she was not human, but a dream woman, seen in a druid mist and a poet passing through the trees at night, with a scattered mind.

The grand people walked into the higher level from side doors. There were gapes and gasps from the audience. The gold and silver and glitter on young, old, fat and scrawny would build a fleet or ransom a king. The silk on back and backside would sail a ship. Last of all Robert Orthega Bollingbrook appeared, waddling like a duck. There was a titter of laughter from the lower deck, soon killed by the clapping of the grand people who could see nothing but nobility in the bloated figure.

——In all me days travelling the roads of Ireland and looking at queer men, I've never seen the likes of him. He's the queerest looking man that ever pulled on a trousers, Foxy Halligan said .to those about him.

——They say he's of the best stock in Ireland and that there is no great name but is associated with him. He has a grand house in Dublin and has been to distant places, a carpenter told Foxy.

——That doesn't add to or take from him, and to the eyes of a man who knows nothing of these things he's only a fart of a man who couldn't piss beyond the toes of his shoes, Foxy Halligan answered back.

There was silence as the company attended the arrival of Kate Houlihan. She appeared at the door in green silk, tight against her body, showing the breeding in every line of her. The grand people smothered their amazement in disciplined silence. But the tinkers, tailors, carpenters, herdsmen, cobblers who had kept her company under ditches, cross-legged on the tables, sawing timber in huts, broke out in uproar. ——Me music to you, Kate, but there is none to compare with you, a voice said.

——Ah Kate, you would woo a man from his travelling on the lonely roads between the small towns, a tinker called.

——For you, Kate, I'd spend a year making a bed as big as a house, of strong joints that would not come undone to the end of the world, a carpenter cried.

——Kate, only the white leather from young lambs is fit for your feet and you walking across polished floors, a shepherd called.

——Silence, roared Mad Houlihan at the rebellion in the cavern. Know your places or I'll set my dogs on you. You are not in a cheap pot house now, rabbling with your drunken friends, he danced in anger.

A voice boomed from the shadows, resonant with authority. ——It is not a custom, nor was it ever, to turn dogs on people. This woman is only receiving the praise and applause she deserves, so let the men be free with their words.

——That's the man with the flair for words and the one to

speak for us, they roared and broke out clapping.

—And who are you to speak out so bravely from the shadows? Houlihan called.

—A harper, juggler, magician deft at my trade and as proud of it as you are of mating animals.

The harper came out of the shadows and walked onto the lighted place prepared for music and entertainment.

—So you're a juggler. Well let us see if you can juggle as well as you can talk, Mad Houlihan guffawed.

He walked up to the dish of fruit in front of Kate. —With your permission? My costume may be shabby, but my hands are white and clean as milk, he said.

She nodded permission.

He threw the plate of fruit into the air and juggled the disorder, his eye glinting right and left. He moved from plate to plate till the mass of fruit mixed into the coloured plumage of the rainbow. All eyes were on the constellation of fruit. He carried it across the floor until he stood before Kate.

—Are you marrying? he asked directly.

—I am.

—To Bollingbrook with the heavy belly?

—Yes.

—There's no comfort in him.

—He'll do.

—I'm a magician and I can see into the mind of any woman.

—What do you see?

—A woman who is condemning herself to open her legs to a man once a year.

—You were listening.

—I'm no listener.

—I've made the choice.

—There is too much music inside you. Only the ugly have to be cold.

—You have a fine tongue.

—I say what's on my mind and on the mind of every tinker, tailor, mason and blacksmith. They don't want you spancelled to that fellow.

—And who are you to talk with such confidence?

——You'll know when I play the harp and you'll see what no one in the room sees.

He moved away from her and plucked the fruit from the whirling tree. Soon the fruit lay in the plates as it had done before O'Leary had juggled.

——Good, good, you're a fair man with your hands, Mad Houlihan said, clapping, and what of the harp?

——I knock music out of it, Harper O'Leary said.

——Well go ahead and do a bit of knocking now.

Harper O'Leary took a stool and placed it in the open space. He planted the harp between his splayed feet and began. It was a slow air like mist creeping over an autumn field with a cargo of dreams. Soon they were all snoring.

——Are you awake Kate? Harper O'Leary asked.

——I am.

——Well what did you see?

——I was pacing the mountains on my white horse with Kelly the man spoken about in all the stores and songs.

——Yes.

——We lived in the quiet places, drinking the water from the clear streams. He caught trout and we baked them over an ash fire. We swam in the morning seas and close to him it was warm.

——Yes.

——Every night he built a sheiling for me and I lay in his arms and he told me all the things a man says to a woman when they lie on the same pillow.

——Yes.

——There is pursuit and we fly from place to place.

——You would go with Kelly?

——Go I would.

——Kate, I'm Kelly.

They rushed from the vaulted room, down the stairs, and out to the stables. They saddled Bawn and rode away. They rode across the mountains and on to Galway until they came to a house by a quiet lake. There they lay together, pillow-talking and making love and slept bodytwined until morning. They ran to the lake and Kate swam close to Kelly across the water.

——Kelly, is it true you swam with dolphins?

——Yes, Kate. I rode on their backs and they led me to the Spanish Gold.

——And Faustus MacGinty and Leibide Ludden, she asked, did they exist?

——They do, the best companions that a man could have.

Later they mounted Bawn which carried them to the Shannon. There on an island they spent the second night, pillow-talking and making love, and fell asleep bound to one another.

Mad Houlihan was the first to wake. He saw Kate's seat empty, the door open.

——Rape, he roared, Kate has been stolen from me. May the sky raise blisters on the head of that harper with his music and magic. Who is the man living who can stray into my castle and steal away my daughter from under my own eyes. I will give ten barrels of gold to the man who will bring him back alive or dead.

——Declare, said Foxy Halligan, but that much gold would bring a man a house, a farm and the finest woman in the parish.

And then a thought came into the mind of Foxy Halligan.

——And with one thing and another that wasn't Harper O'Leary, but Kelly, the greatest cut-throat and thief in the country, he roared.

——Not the Kelly that's playing havoc with every girl in the country? Mad Houlihan asked.

——The very same, Foxy said.

——If he's let, he'll destroy the stock of the country. The race will weaken under him, Houlihan complained.

——We have scores to settle with him, for he killed my father and maimed half the tribe, Foxy Halligan told the gathering.

——Ten more barrels of gold, Houlihan said, to the man that brings back my daughter.

——After him before the winter sets in, Foxy said.

They streamed out the door like bees swarming from a hive. The grand people got into their carriages and on their horses, the tinkers into their carts and away they went down every road in Ireland.

Except Mad Houlihan and Foxy Halligan.

—He'll outsmart them because he's a smart man. One must think and plan, Foxy Halligan said, for you cannot tangle with him in a fair fight, we must steal up on him and knife him.

—But when? Mad Houlihan asked.

—One time only. When he's weak with love. I think that like the great whale who has his own way in the sea, he'll head back to Belmullet and out to Duvillaun Island where he ate the gulls' eggs and stole the Spanish gold, Foxy Halligan said.

—We'll go north and wait for him, even if it takes all winter, Mad Houlihan told him.

—Take ten of your best men and we'll go with you, Foxy Halligan said.

And while the rest went in chase of Kelly, Foxy Halligan and Mad Houlihan went north in easy steps. They carried food to the island and waited. Three months they waited, the snow blowing hard, the seas angry and churly, the sky low running, nature dead. In spring, looking over towards Fallmore, they saw a boat approaching. Kelly was rowing with easy strokes. Kate sitting in the back, trailing fingers in the water.

Their laughter rang like silver bells.

They sailed towards the trap. All day eyes were on them from the rocks as they played on the sand and swam naked in the seas. Fury, hunger foiled behind the eyes of the watchers. Night came easy and Kelly lit a fire. He broiled fish for Kate, carried cool water for her in his cupped hands, deftly made a small sheiling where they lay together. They watched as Kate and Kelly tumbled and laughed.

Later Kelly lay exhausted, away from Kate, breathing in the sweet air.

Then they were upon him, with knives, cutting at his body, tearing at his eyes, throttling his neck, trying to pull out his wind pipe. Mad Houlihan, knife in hand, moved around the mass of marauding figures.

—Where are his nuts, where are his nuts until I geld him? he roared.

Kelly twitched with pain as they drove the knives into his

body and clawed at his neck. They were pounding his face
with their boots, beating his skull. He gathered all his remaining strength and heaved them from him. He ran bleeding
along the beach.

He was weakening. He felt death hover like an ugly crow.

And while Mad Houlihan and the frenzied Halligans were
bent upon cooperative revenge, Kate ran up the beach away
from the angers and the hate. She tore her feet on sharp shell
fragments. Her flight was noted by one of the Halligans who
broke from the mad tangle. His blood lust was broken at the
sight of her white body. He ran in pursuit. She dashed among
the dunes, a labyrinth of rabbit tracks, the bull presence of
the man everywhere. As she escaped out of the maze on to
the sea shore, he was there fronting her and she knew that
an end had come to the flight and the chase. Kelly, no longer
proud, tongueless perhaps, would die on the far beach she
thought. His blood would be otter drink, his bones would be
picked by birds and island rats. She would be led back to the
tower. There was an end to everything.

But then across the sea and out of the evening galloped
Lubach Caol, sparks flying from sea pebbles as he dashed
towards Kate Houlihan and the dark figure of the tinker who
was upon her. Lubach Caol's eyes burned furnace red. He
snapped and kicked at the tinker, who ran from the wild and
mythical horse. Now there was only the sound of shore waves
on the sand. The horse nudged Kate with his nose. She rose
and dragged herself onto his mangey back.

On the far side of the narrow, ell long island, Kelly knew
that death was near. He had been overbold, overproud and
an over-reacher. His white god skin was netted with knife
cuts. He weakened and fell on the stones. His enemies could
now have their revenge.

But as they bore down upon him he heard horse hoof
sounds. He looked up and saw Lubach Caol, Kate upon his
back, coming towards him. A final strength surged through
his body. He drew himself up from the stones and staggered
towards Kate and Lubach Caol.

——I was almost done, Kate, he cried as she bent down to
pull him onto the horse. I thought the tide had turned

against me as it does for all mortal men.

He dragged himself onto the horse. His enemies were about him, the horse snapping at them with his old yellow teeth. They would surely drag Kelly down again.

But then a strange thing happened. Lubach Caol became a horse of gold. Strong wings grew from its shoulders and it bore Kate and Kelly out over the sea and up towards the stars and away from it all.